The Caretaker

Cass Clarke

Copyright © 2023 Cass Clarke

All rights reserved.

ISBN: 978-0-6452355-4-8

DEDICATION

I dedicate this book to my dad, who never questioned *if* I'd be a published author but always asked *when*. He didn't live to see this moment, but I like to think he's tapping away a letter to me on his keyboard somewhere, and somehow that message will find its way to me when I need it most. Here's looking at you, kid.

"Each sentence of The Caregiver pries open your chest, resulting in an ache that leaves you hoping the next page stitches it right back up. Clarke's storytelling is instinctual and earnest. A merciless journey of a read." – Blayne Waterloo, *Fangoria*.

"Cass Clarke's novella is a powerful portrait of grief forged in a crucible of terrors. It blazes with humanness and fiercely burns for the transmutation of pain in the most shocking and also loving ways. There is humor, horror, and healing here. A great, sometimes sexy, and often gruesome read that chips away, cracked nails and all, at what it means to love, be loved, and let go." – Toby Poser, *Adams Family Films*.

"Cass Clarke's The Caregiver is a chilling nightmare that gets to the core of my deepest fear. Equal parts terrifying and heart-breaking, Clarke beautifully imbues the novella with a deep sense of empathy that makes its horrors all the more devastating." – Mary Beth McAndrews, *Dread Central*

"There's a delicious ache that comes in the aftermath of being startled by images and emotions that sneak up on you when you weren't expecting them. That ache...? That ache is "The Caretaker". In this novella, Clarke has managed to wrap up stark imagery and poignant evocations of feelings that don't want to be remembered within an allegory of motherhood and caretaking that will ache long after you're done reading." – R.J. Joseph, award winning, Stoker™ and Shirley Jackson awards nominated writer.

CONTENTS

1	What We Leave Behind	1
2	What We Choose to Keep	12
3	Those Who Choose to Stay	22
4	Those Who Dare Return	28
5	The One Who's Always There	36
6	The One Who Answered	44
7	What We Have to Lose	52
8	Who She Used to Be	60
9	The Play-Pen	68
10	A Loss too Big to Name	77
11	The One Who Listens	84
12	What's Left to Say	94
Epilogue	How We Carry On	105

Content Warning

Dementia/Alzheimer's
Grief
PTSD
Disassociation
Depression
Domestic violence

WHAT WE LEAVE BEHIND

Cara

At my mother's wake, a neighbor I haven't seen in years, tells me, "She was a wonderful woman." *Pfft*. You'd think in death my mother would *finally* be demoted to obscurity. A woman. Some woman. "A devoted nurse" they say. With each passing handshake, I bite my bottom lip harder. The iron taste of blood helps. It reminds me I'm alive. I hold the power now. Each person has an empty platitude to gift me. Some planted trees in her memory. I nod and say thank you, though it's a lie—all of this. All they want is to put on a good show. After the assembly line of wishing me well ends, the folks who stay sit in foldout chairs aligned in neat rows in front of me. They stare like I'm a wild animal on display: *Here lies ungrateful daughter, don't touch, she will bite.* Behind me, an antique clock hangs from the wood-paneled walls, announcing each agonizing second of this morbid display—*tick, tick, tick*. Two hours to go. Jesus. I sit silently, watching how we Irish Catholics grieve: gossiping, headshaking, and refusing to cry—unless shots are on the table, and no one can see the breaking.

Relatives I only see at births, funerals, and weddings pass the time chattering about Trump politics and last night's bar tabs. No one wants to look at the body. I imagine how it'd feel to scream like a banshee until they shut their goddamn mouths. Instead, I dig my fingernails into my palms, as if this will keep me from falling apart. Every fiber of my being wants me to let go, fall to my knees, and wail. But I won't. Not here. Not now. I won't give them the satisfaction of a story to tell on the ride home. I won't give *her*, of all people, the privilege. I grind my heels into the kaleidoscope-colored carpet that hasn't been changed since the '70s, listening to their aimless conversations. They're filling time. Too afraid to ask, how many minutes equal enough sympathy?

Everyone is waiting for someone else to kneel first. I start, so others will follow. I'll give the Mansfield Funeral Home this, they did her hair better than she had in years. Her thick brown locks cling to her sunken cheekbones as if she commanded those too to fit her infinite demands. Pale lips stretched into a thin line, sculpted into a forced smile. In her iron-clad grip is the black-beaded rosary she used to wear. "One more little thing," she'd tell me. But it was never one thing nor a little ask. I press my hand to her forehead, cold as marble.

Enough. I stand to make room for the others, finally lining up, to say their peace and leave, so this can all be done, so I can go home and put on my scrubs and be hands deep in intestines and blood vessels the stuff that makes sense. Rewiring bodies back into being, into the right shapes, into someone stitched anew.

"Her memory will linger on," a cousin says.

"That's what I'm afraid of…"

***

If anyone heard me say it, they pretended otherwise. But I had every right to be afraid. It was only just beginning. I couldn't have known it, in those days as rough as rawhide, but she left me another mess to fix.

***

Lately, there had been so many arrangements. When I return to my mother's home, it hits me that I still have to deal with her hospice bed. There it is in the living room, an adjustable mauve mattress. Still, the bed held her body's outline like an unearthed fossil. Seeing it gave me flashes of the worst of it—her final days alive.

Days ago, she wheezed and coughed up knotted clots of tissue, years of chain-smoking cigarettes caught up to her. Rattling breath. Hands tinted blue. Skin thin as tissue paper. Purple veins unfurled the worn roadmap of her body. I want to set the bed on fire. Burn the smell of rotting bedsores that still fills the room. A patch of flesh on her right thigh turned black as coal, flaking on the sheets, as if she was preparing to become nothing but ash. We used to eat dinner in this room, watching some sitcom as she drank too much wine and bemoaned all that was—a strange place to watch her die, but it was the most accessible entry point for hospice. By the time I found her, speaking was off the table. I hadn't talked to her in months and when I visited; she was on the floor, moaning. I don't know how much of me she felt in the end. Her eyes barely opened. Food had no purpose. Oh, the moaning. I still hear it when I close my eyes. That sound will live in me forever. When hospice asked why I hadn't called sooner, I had no words. Nothing would make them understand how it was with her.

My phone rings, snapping me out of the spiral.

Most people don't know this but when hospice arrives, they don't bring a new bed. Whatever bed comes has just left a home where someone died. There's no way to know how many people said goodbye on that mattress before you. No measure for that colossal weight. After the passing, there always comes the collection.

Well, that's how it's supposed to work. I want nothing more than to get rid of this fucking thing. But I keep playing phone tag with Susan, my mom's former hospice nurse. In three days, I've left five voicemails.

"About time, Susan."

"Cara," she says. "I'm so sorry but we're short-staffed. I won't be able to pick up the bed until next week." Well, fuck you very much, Susan. Just what I need on today of all days—another night with *it*.

"Text when you're coming. You know, I have a job to get back to."

"Of course," she said. "Just, stay clear of it. It can be hard with all the memories it brings."

"Fine."

"...Are you ok? You know we have services you can talk to if you —"

I hang up the phone.

***

If Susan knew the truth about the bed, she never told me. Then again, I never asked.

***

After the wake, I move from room to room like a whisper of a being. Flittering from place to place with no intent or why. When the doorbell rings, I almost forgot what that meant, someone's here. I open the door, but no one's on the stone steps. Strange. But I'd be lying if I said I wasn't relieved. There is so much talking in the early days of grief from *everyone*. I have no idea what to say or how or when. Despite people telling you that you can reach them at any time and chat, the idea of doing so feels like climbing an impossible cliff. I haven't the strength nor experience of losing a parent to know how to chart this terrain. I never knew my father—some one-night fling in nursing school history—so this is my one and only time to stumble through it all. I used to think it'd make me lucky. Like I'd only have to feel a loss like this once in my life. But now I know I was wrong.

All I hear are my footsteps alone in a house turned upside down with clutter, dust, and enveloping silence.

Two weeks, that'll be all it'll take for me to settle up this house. After, I'll sell it off and all the junk. That's all this is. Nothing more and nothing less—a way to pay off my nursing school loans and have a nest egg for whatever it is I'm supposed to have one for? Stocks? A mortgage? Never really got that far in my life plans.

I pour a glass of red wine and stare at the bed, transfixed by what it no longer held. I know, I know I'm not supposed to look at it. But that just makes me want to do it more. I resist the urge to take a butcher knife to it, slicing its seams—pulling the fluff out of it like a rabid dog with sinew in its teeth. I imagine all the ways I could destroy it, as if in some way I too would be destroying her. I never even got the chance to do that right.

Again, the doorbell rings. I look at my phone: 11:00 PM? Late for the suburbs. I open the door, but no one is there. No car parked on our cul-de-sac road. All the surrounding ranch houses have their curtains closed. There's only the dim light of the streetlamp flickering on and off, casting a yellow haze into a starless sky.

When I return to the living room, something is different. The bed had moved. Not much. Just an inch or so. The windows are open, *and* the bed has wheels. I chalk it up to a timely gust of wind and uneven flooring.

***

That was my first mistake.

***

At 3:00 AM, I feel someone watching me sleep. I open my eyes and see a shadow lingering near my bed. I squint and make out the outline of my robe on a chair. I'm just tired. That's all. But then it moves. A black cloud hovers near my nightstand and moves closer to me. Closer, closer, it floats above my face, then lowering closer and closer to my lips. I clench my eyes shut as if it'd make me or that thing or this dream disappear.

When I open my eyes, it's somehow 8:00 AM. There's nothing and no one around me. I know I only closed my eyes for a second. No way I drank *that* much, right? Maybe Susan was right and I'm "processing" it all. She told me that in the days after someone dies, the living move like zombies. I don't think that's true at all. Zombies have an appetite. They crave the taste of life. I, on the other hand, hunger for nothing like want.

***

This was the start of the visits. The longer I stayed, the longer they were summing me up. Was I anything like my mother? A question I had asked myself countless times but never knew they'd care. Oh, they'll care. How much? Tortuous amounts. What had they to lose? She already took everything from them.

***

Today is the funeral mass. Unlike the wake, I can't get away with sitting in silence. I have to speak in this cavernous church and make some meaning about her life aloud. There's nothing I'm wishing for more than my phone buzzing with a three-car pileup and a request for me to pick up a shift. Dark, I know. But it's honest.

I never planned to follow in my mother's footsteps and become a nurse. But after a childhood of making cue cards for each CNA and RNA course, I gained so much of a leg up that it felt silly not to do it. But there was one crucial difference: she worked in geriatric care, and I work in the ER. She prepared those for death as I prepared those to live as full a life as possible after the unexpected trauma sidewipes their lives head-on.

I chase the buzz of the beeper and call signs, savoring each potential distraction and its promise of helping others. My mother prided herself in being able to estimate the exact time someone would die. We are not the same. Something I have to tell myself daily. Though I wish I didn't have to.

At the church, too many relatives ask to be pallbearers. I assign the three tallest cousins at random. I turn and am relieved to see the only cousin I actually talk to, Dylan, standing by his truck. He knows me best; knows I'll talk to him when I'm ready. He won't add to the performative fanfare, the awkward back-patting, and small talk. I excuse myself from the gaggle of aunts and uncles and give him a hug. He squeezes me tight as a grizzly bear. But I don't mind the pressure. I like the idea that he's somehow pushing pieces of me back into place, resetting the shifts in my bones I can't feel yet. All my jagged edges softened. I stop holding my breath.

"Thank fucking god," I say.

"I know," Dylan says. "This is gonna suck, but this will be the hardest part."

I trust Dylan when he says this. Years ago, he lost his mother. He was much younger than me. In my 30s, this sucks, but I've had enough life before being torpedoed. He was 12. I'm not mad he didn't show up to the wake. Our mothers were sisters born a year apart and looked like twins. That would have been too hard. Unlike me, Dylan thought his mom was the coolest person in the world. As a lounge singer, she kinda was.

"You look nice," I say.

"Oh, this old thing?" he says, smirking. He's wearing a dark suit whereas everyone else chose jeans or a run-of-the-mill blouse. I can tell he added extra beard oil today and ironed his shirt. A burly man, Dylan isn't one to do things in half-measures or show up unless he wants to be there. For that, for him, I'm grateful.

"Let the charade begin."

***

I know I did the readings. I know I gave a eulogy. But somewhere between walking down the aisle and staring at the stained glass, rearranging the shards of color into howling faces, I disappeared. All I remember is the thick smell of burning incense clouding the room, as a priest spoke in a dead language—as if we weren't good enough to hear his words to God about my mother. Sobbing, yes, but not from me. My eyes filled with tears that refused to fall as Auntie Lee—who hadn't seen my mother in a decade—cried the loudest of us all.

Though, I do remember how the entire church turned to stare at me when my work beeper went off. Miriam Hospital could only go two days before asking me to pick up a night shift. I texted back, "We'll see."

After everyone else leaves, Dylan flags me over to his truck in the parking lot. The surrounding elm trees have lost most of their leaves, so each step closer to him brings a satisfying crunch like cracking knuckles.

"Want to go for a drink?" he asks.

"It's 2:00 PM."

"Eh, what else do you have to do today?"

"Well… work messaged me."

"Cara, your mom just died. That's the last thing you should be thinking about…"

"It's not like one shift is a big deal."

"Oh, you know it won't go like that. First, it's this, then I lose you for weeks…What about the burial? Shouldn't we be getting to that soon? If you need a ride, I can take you there. Whatever you need, Cara."

I shake my head. "Priest is taking care of it. I'm not going."

"Ok, ok…well what if we go to PJ's? C'mon, you know it's your favorite… pretty please?"

"Fine…just stop looking at me like that, *and* the tabs on you."

"Bring on the fried pickles!"

"I will drink that spicy mayo and you can't say shit about it today."

"I'll get you a pint glass of it," Dylan says, unleashing a bellowing laugh. He swings his arm around me. Another tight squeeze. Another reminder to stop holding my breath. For now, I turn my beeper to silent.

As he drives us in his rusty Ford pick-up, I find the scratching sounds of jostled lawnmowers and hedge clippers in his truck bed strangely soothing. I crack open the window and let the winter chill spread over my bones. Dusk falls. We pass old railroad tracks and the Providence River until we're in a section of downtown where all the run-down mills have been turned into trendy bars with overpriced french fries. Not our thing. PJ's feels grimy—the good kind—with heavy-handed pours, glitchy lighting, and boxed arcade games about aliens.

"Lee is something, huh?" Dylan says, breaking the thick silence between us.

"She does that at *every* funeral."

"Did you time it this time?"

"Godammit! I forgot." I slam my hand on his dashboard littered with unpaid parking tickets, straw wrappers, and a Tom Brady bobblehead. "Definitely more than Uncle Bobby's… uhh, twenty minutes?"

"I got you," he says. "Thirty-two minutes and ten seconds."

I laugh for the first time all month. I forgot I could make a sound like that, and it startles me as if hearing myself speak fluently in a foreign language. I don't want it to stop but it does. Of course, the quiet returns.

"At least she didn't try to arrange the whole funeral like when Uncle Tommy died," Dylan says, jabbing his elbow into my side. "Can you imagine picking out caskets with that one? You'd go bankrupt."

"Trust me, she tried," I said. "I just didn't answer her texts."

"Ha! Knew it. Can never leave well enough alone, that one."

We drive up a steep hill and turn down a cobblestone alley that makes his truck jiggle. We find a good spot close to the entrance of PJ's. Dylan opens the door and the rusty dive bar sign creaks in the darkness. I know I'm supposed to move but can't bring myself to open the door. Dylan opens it for me, thankfully.

"Cara, what is it? You've barely spoken to me. You can, you know?"

"I know, I know. It's...nothing. Just thinking about something."

"Well, what is it? Nothing or something?"

I sigh, "I don't know, losing time...It's weird. When, you know... did this happen to you?"

Dylan exhales, parsing through what I asked. Even after two decades, it's still a delicate subject to bring up, to ask someone to rifle through boxed-up memories of their hardest loss to give you any comfort at all.

"Depends," he says. "For me, time moved slowly. Minutes felt like hours. I did all I could to fill that time with stuff—anything, any errand, or an excuse just to do something with my hands. Not sit still in all... that."

"Oh."

"Is that what you mean?"

"No, it's different. It's like someone pressed the fast-forward button. One moment I'm in a room and then in the blink of an eye, it's been hours of me sitting there or lying down on a bed. Does that make sense?"

"Hm."

"Hm?"

"That's all I got to say right now. This stuff doesn't have a road map, kiddo." Dylan is only six years older than me, but he's been calling me kiddo since he was eight. "But you won't be getting rid of me too easily. Landscaping jobs are slow in December, so I'll be around. You took some time off from work, right? Right?"

"Yes, yes. Two weeks."

"Good, don't go picking up more shifts on the sly either. Take care of yourself."

"Okay, okay, let's get a drink."

"Oh, you can have more than a drink today with me. I'll be insulted if you don't."

I had too many. At *PJ's Bar*, with Dylan, time moved differently. Not quite at normal speed, but something closer to that. As we threw darts, I counted each one that landed. I knew how many rounds we played—four. We ate fried pickles and fries. Measurable things. Tangible things. He anchored me as waves of grief crashed and retreated. The push and pull of sorrow and numbness competed for my attention. But in this space, neither won. Seconds passed without me remembering what day was today. I loved this here and now.

Dylan was right. It had been ages since we hung out. I needed this. I needed him. We were both only children, so this is the closest we got to siblings. Losing our mothers only made it more obvious to both of us.

***

If he had known what was to come, would he still have helped me? Would I have let him?

WHAT WE CHOOSE TO KEEP

Cara

Cleaning out your childhood home feels like winning a reverse lottery; your job, which no one else wants to do, is to get rid of as many things as possible. But there are just so many things in a home. The things have things! Looking at the mountainous volume of bills on the table and the unwashed dishes caked with food in the broken dishwasher, I'm regretting that fifth round of IPAs with Dylan. I stumble my way to the pantry filled with haphazardly stacked pans to find the coffee pot. I brew enough to jumpstart my mushy brain.

During the hospice days, I commuted between here and my apartment. I came and left, relishing all the things that weren't my job to consider. The joke is on me though—now I have to handle all she left undone.

Figures. Wasn't that how it always was with her?

I find the least dirty mug in the cupboard, which is still covered in some dusty grime. I choose to ignore it. I swing back a cup of black coffee, and send Dylan a text: *Uh, what do you know about dishwashers?*

He replies: *Enough to tell you don't touch anything until I'm there in an hour.*

Fair enough. The house is in complete disarray. I need all the help I can get. I knew sorting through things would be hard, but I severely underestimated how tired I'd feel. God, it's like I've been shadowboxing for days. I *know* we're not supposed to discuss diseases or grief like they're wars on some battlefield. Strength and patience cannot prevail over a tumor's grasp if it's that person's time to go. I tell my patients that all the time. But if I'm honest, I don't believe it. Who can? In the last few weeks at home with my mother, I couldn't stop counting the losses to come—her crackling laugh, the sting of her backhanded compliments, the smell of Dove's body soap mixed with disinfectant wipes. Every day by her bedside brought a hundred new goodbyes to name. How can you not feel like the illness won when tallying up the score of all that's been taken from you?

I can't.

In the bathroom, the towels are dry and brittle. Before becoming bedridden, my mother became obsessed with the idea of saving, for what or for whom, I don't fucking know, as if every light switch flipped on or cycle in the dryer took essential money and time from her. She decided to air-dry towels in the basement, so now they make a crinkly sound when folded. Of all the tasks to do, this is where I began—ugh, laundry.

Before Dylan arrives, I've done two loads with endless rounds to go in the dimly lit and musky cellar. There's only one lamp down here, which makes it all needlessly difficult. Of course, I trip on a cracked floor tile; spilling a basket onto the floor. Some towels scatter under the rusty washer. *Motherfucker.* On my knees, I slide my fingers underneath the metal crevice, covering my mouth and nose with my other hand. The smell is putrid. I'm glad I can't see what else is under here, as I wouldn't be surprised to find a litter of small dead things. Caked dirt makes the white tiles a greasy grey. If this was a horror movie, this would be when a hand would grasp my wrist, pulling me into shadowy depths. Ah, there. I pull out two pink towels covered in dust and throw them into the garbage. No way I'm cleaning that. Out of nowhere, a cool breeze slides across the nape of my neck. My back straightens like someone pulled a rip cord at the base of my spine. There are no windows down here.

Nothing is there Cara. Still, my heart jolts like a jackrabbit, readied to hide in the thickest brush. I grab the basket, but I can't move. For a moment, I glimpse something black in the corner of my eyes, lingering in my peripheral vision, a smudge. I count to three and turn to face whatever it is. But it fades into the shadows of the room behind old skis. Still, I sense it. Watching. This is the point where you don't step forward, don't look closer. But I'm tired of always doing what I'm supposed to do. Someone behind me grips my shoulder tight.

I scream, dropping the basket onto the floor.

"Woah, Cara," Dylan said.

"Jesus-fucking-Christ!"

"You ok? I rang the doorbell. Didn't you hear it?"

"No, no, I think it might be broken?... What else is new around here." I bend down and pick up the scattered towels, shaking out the dust from them before tossing them unfolded into the wicker basket.

"You left the door unlocked."

"I'm fine. Not like a toddler or a 70-year-old is gonna rob me in this neighborhood."

"Huh, this place has... changed a lot since I've been here?"

Dylan is too nice to say shit-show. Like his judgment of this place will somehow reflect poorly on me. But I can tell he's thinking it. He rolls his flannel sleeves up and helps me gather the remaining towels.

"Everything is just... everything." With a shake of the head, I add, "I'll figure it out, don't worry. I always do. Might even buy you a shiny new truck once I sell this place to some straight breeders."

"One, how dare you, Redd is doing just fine. Two, I mean, you're gonna hate me saying this but… "

"Then why say it?"

"She has other family… Can't they fuck around with garage sales or something?"

"Dylan, you know how our family is. And do you see them anywhere? Did any of *them* think of calling hospice or visiting me? No, no they all like to talk shit about how I left her, but did anyone dare to stay here?" I can feel my words leaving my lips like a thousand tiny blades, cutting directly into Dylan. "I'm…I'm sorry."

"It's ok, it's ok…I know you don't mean me. Here, let me grab the baskets."

Before going upstairs, my eyes linger on the skis. Maybe it's best to leave darkness alone.

***

For years, I ignored the darkness in this house. Soon, it'll be the darkness' turn to push me aside.

***

After about an hour of fiddling with the dishwasher's wires and wheels, Dylan asks for a screwdriver. When he asks why I'm going to my mother's bedroom, I handwave him away. My mother had this way of remembering everything's proper place—even if it was unanimously out of place. A screwdriver? Time to open her armoire! The second drawer near her socks is where it'd be, but the drawer won't open. I holler for Dylan.

"There's something stuck in the ball bearing's way," he says.

"It's cute that you think I know what a ball bearing is."

"You can assist with a lung surgery, but you can't identify parts of a drawer?"

"I have girlfriends for that."

He snorts. "Yeah, that's probably why they don't stick around long."

"Hey!" I swat his back, accidentally pushing him into the drawer. But that little nudge slips his wedged hand deeper, pushing out a piece of a manilla folder. "There it is! Pull that. What the hell is this now?"

"Hold on, hold on… Ok, got it!"

I snatch the folder from his hand.

"A thanks would be nice?"

"Playing the dead parent card… What? Don't give me that look."

"I'm too hungover to argue," Dylan says, rubbing his temples. "What is it?"

Inside, there are a lot of receipts that make no sense to me. Underneath all that, there are several photos. I don't recognize these people, but I see my mother with a stethoscope around her pale neck in each shot.

"Oh, I think it's her patients? But…Why just keep photos of these ones?"

"I don't know. Her favorites, I guess?"

"Huh."

"What?"

"Nothing."

"Cara."

"It's just, why keep them hidden? Not like it's a secret to me that she liked her patients more."

"Maybe she forgot they were there? Let's just put these down. Now might not be the best—"

Too late. I grab a photo at random, some old man I don't know sits next to her as they smile and drink tea. On the back of the photo, my mom's scrawled handwriting— *Oliver & Me, 2000.* I rip them in halves and thirds and fourths until the two are nothing more than floating heads scattered across the hardwood floor.

"Was that really necessary?"

"It's the least I'm deserved."

"Ok."

"Ok?"

"If that's what you need, it's what you need."

A crash echoes through the house. We run towards the sound in the kitchen. Maybe that Jenga of a pantry finally gave up holding itself together too? In the hallway, there it is again. That black spot in my vision rushing around me each time I turn my head so I can't get a proper look. "Dylan, did you see that?"

"See what?"

"Wait, what the hell?"

We stop dead in our tracks. Dylan nudges me back.

"Stay here, Cara."

"The fuck I will," I say, swatting his arm away.

In the kitchen, the cupboard door is on the floor, looking like someone cracked it in half. We walk over to the door, surveying the scattered splinters on the floor. A smoky black blur rushes past my left side. Plates rattle inside the cupboard. Dylan bends down and grazes the cracked wood with his callused fingers. In the cupboard, a tower of dishes teeters against the edge. No. I pull Dylan by his neckline away from the mess. "The fuck," he says, but stops when the plates shatter against the emerald tile floor. We fall backward in disbelief.

"How did you?"

"I saw —"

But then the dishwasher's door slams on the ground, breaking off from the machine as if an invisible hand tore and twisted the sheet metal like it was nothing thicker or heavier than paper. Dylan pulls me so close I can smell his peppery vanilla aftershave and hear his pounding heart. "That's…not possible," he whispers.

"This is more than just old hinges and worn-down

stuff, right? Do you think..."

"Let's get out of this death trap for a while, ok? I need some air...and beer."

"*PJ's?*"

"*PJ's.*"

At 3:00 PM on a Sunday, we're sandwiched at the sticky bar between couples who love watching football and bored wives who love texting while their husbands talk at them. Least it's loud enough that no one hears me say words like "dead mom" or "my haunted house." I order a scotch and bury my head in my hands.

"Cara? You ok?"

"Dylan," I say without looking up. "That was weird, right?"

"Uh, yeah," he says, taking a sip from his beer. "Pretty sure cupboards don't naturally shred themselves up like that last time I checked. Or dishwashers. Boy, you never make things easy on me, do you?"

"Rude."

"But honest."

He's not wrong. I take a sip from my scotch, savoring how it takes like wood lacquer burning the back of my throat. "I saw a black fog. I thought it was just from not sleeping that much. But...I don't know."

"Uh, I do," he says. "I was there. This isn't some weird dream. People always say dumb things like that in scary movies and guess what happens? That sucker is the first one to get gutted like a fish, and I am no fish."

"You really need to stop quoting *Scream*."

"Tell me, I'm wrong then?"

I fiddle with my phone, debating if I should call the one person who'd have any experience with this kind of stuff. That's exactly what your ex-girlfriend wants to hear: *Hey, Beth, I know it's been ages, but can you drive an hour to help me cleanse my dead mom's house? I think it wants to kill me. Oh yeah, how are you doing?* Instead, I swing back the rest of my scotch and order a third round. "Hear me out. What if it was Oliver?"

"Who?"

"That photo I tore up, had the name Oliver written on it. I guess he must have been a patient of my mom's. What if I pissed him off somehow? Remember that time in *Supernatural* when Bobby—"

"—Ok, give me a second to catch up if we're gonna talk about that dumb show *again*." Dylan switches from IPAs to tequila, a choice he always regrets. Yet, he'll still order it and ask me why in the morning.

"It's universally beloved!"

"Nah, people just like hot dudes."

"Oh, that so?"

"I can appreciate the male form, ok? Not my style but c'mon…I'm not blind."

"We're gonna unpack that later. But anyways, they burn objects that contain someone's essence. Maybe that photo has a bit of leftover Oliver in it. Maybe I pissed him off somehow and we gotta burn it?"

"How do you know he's dead?"

"He was like 100 in that photo and that was taken 20 years ago."

Dylan slams his hand on the bar.

"Woah, what I say?"

Dylan shakes his head. "Nah, just the Pats fumbled. Never shoulda let Brady go."

"Dylan! Are you serious right now?"

"Hey, I can multitask," he says, slamming back a shot. "Besides this might be the last game I watch if things are going any way, you're thinking they're going. What a season to go out on, am I right?"

"Oh my god, we would so die in *Supernatural*."

"Yeah, but you don't resurrect 500 times in the real

world," he says, knocking back another shot and slamming it on the bar so the empty glasses rattle against the wood. "Don't forget that. Only get one go of it."

"So you *do* watch the show. I knew it!"

"Figures, that's what you take from that," he sighs. "Lucky, I love ya… Oh, c'mon, Jones! You got fingers made of hot dogs?… What? I do see *some* of the movies you talk about. Plus, Michelle Yeoh is a hottie."

"Can't argue there."

Against my better judgment, I send Beth a text. I decide to leave out, well, everything. I don't mention it to Dylan because he's not a guy who believes in "crystal healing." Besides, what harm can one little hey do?

Back home and *very* drunk, Dylan and I pick up the scraps of Oliver's photo from my mother's bedroom. We burn the remnants in the sink. I watch how the flames encircle the edges, devouring their image from the outside in until there's nothing left but their smiling faces collapsing into their charred remains.

"This has to work, right?" I ask.

"Why are you even doing this? The house, *this*, you didn't even like your mom." He'd never ask me this if he was sober. He knew some of it, not all of it. No one really did, except for my Beth—and I wish she hadn't.

"I just am, ok? You won't understand."

"Won't I? What if it doesn't work, huh? What will you do? How much will you put up with?"

"I'm tired, Dylan."

He sighs and adds, "Okay, okay, it's too soon. I get it."

"Thank you."

"All I'm saying is this is nuts, Cara! You can just leave. All of it. C'mon. Your mother is gone. You don't owe her anything anymore. She can't say shit to you. You can do whatever you want. Do you get that?"

"Back off, Dylan. I swear to God." The acidic sting of my words silences him. "I don't want to talk about it. It's been what? Two-ish days since she died? You said so yourself. Let me do what I need. OK?"

We each take a couch in the living room, dropping the topic for now, even if it does mean I have to stare at that fucking bed. I lie awake to Dylan's snoring. I keep my phone ringer on in case Beth texts back, though she doesn't. I turn my work beeper back on—though I know I shouldn't. But we all need our escape hatches, right? Before long, I fall into a fitful sleep, tossing and turning, cocooning myself in blankets.

***

Deep down, I knew this would never be easy. But I wanted to prove I could outlive this home. Emptying out each nook and polishing each crevice, these things soothed me. I thought if I could break it all down into individual parts and scrub away all that was, I'd leave who I was with it. That lonely and broken version of Cara would rest, for good. That Cara could lock the front door and never return. But I never got that far.

THOSE WHO CHOOSE TO STAY

Cara

The black smoke returns, hovering above my body. Of all the ways to go, I'd never thought it'd be like this; likely something sadder like choking on a potato chip alone in my apartment. Again, I want to move but it's as if whatever tied my brain to my body has been severed. I just lie there as the dark smoky substance comes closer. This time it's not quite without a shape, forming the outline of Oliver's body moving slowly, ever so slowly toward me—savoring how fast my heart beats, how I'm trying so hard to scream but my tongue has glued itself inside my mouth. Please. Oliver doesn't give a shit. The man's face isn't there, but I know he's watching me and has been for some time. Closer, and closer he approaches. His head is now inches from my mouth. He leans further in, pressing against my lips until he pushes through and the space between our bodies disappears. He's pouring himself down my throat. I can't stop it. I'm choking, but I can't breathe enough to make a sound.

Words that aren't mine float into my head; *You shouldn't have done that.*

My throat bulges wide and my jaw unhinges like a snake swallowing a mouse. The black smoke slithers deeper into my body, increasing its speed and pressure on my insides. My clavicle breaks under the pulsating weight of it, and so do my ribcages—as the darkness spreads and spreads into each corner of me. I can't lift my hand or head or body, though I try, the flood of nothingness tries harder, and I'm paralyzed by its power.

Dylan throws a pillow at my face, waking me up.

"Stop screaming," he says. "*Ugh*, why did I have to have tequila…"

It takes a couple of seconds for my brain to catch up. "This was a dream. But what happened before wasn't, right?" I ask, despite knowing that Dylan is too dead to the world right now to do much than grunt. "Do you think the photo thing worked? Dylan? Dylan… c'mon, wake up." I throw a pillow back at him.

Before Dylan can answer, the doorbell rings. Still in last night's clothes with sweaty palms and my brain feeling like it's being crushed under boulders, I answer the door. "Oh, hi, Auntie Lee," I say loud enough for Dylan to hear. I hear his groan, as Auntie Lee invites herself in with a tuna fish casserole in hand and already talking a mile a minute. She's who Charles Schulz probably imagined when he decided all adults sound like a muted trombone. Her behemoth of a handbag chatters with keychains of silver angels. All the clattering sounds make my headache worsen. I nod and smile at whatever she's talking about like I'm listening. But all I hear is *mwah, mwah, mwah*.

"You didn't answer me," Auntie Lee says, tapping her acrylic nails on a nearby table.

"I really appreciate you stopping by," I lie.

"Auntie Lee!"

Dylan swoops in to relieve me. Bless him. We move into the dining room. I heat up her dish and put out a serving for each of us at the end of the dining room table—sweeping the piles of untended things to the side. Auntie Lee squints at the stack of mail, judging the mess. Ugh, my stomach contorts at the fishy smell.

"Well, you're so big now, Dylan! I bet you could lift me up," she says.

"With one hand, probably," Dylan says, scarfing down the food. Bits of tuna fall on his shirt with each bite he takes. God, I'm gonna puke. When I do, it's going right into her dumb handbag. Swear to God.

"Ok, well, thank you for the visit but I think I need some rest," I say, getting up from the table and hurrying to clear the dishes, even though Dylan had just scooped a second helping onto his plate.

"You haven't even had a bite!" Auntie Lee says. "You're too thin. You gotta eat more."

"I'm good," I say. "Really."

"Well, let me help you clean up," she says, following me to the kitchen. "Looks like you need help."

"Oh no, that's ok—" but she barrels ahead of me anyways. This fuckin' family.

"What in the world! What did you do to the dishwasher?"

"Oh, um…We're replacing the door," I say.

"So, in the meantime, you left the broken door on the floor? Honey, are you *sure* you don't need some help? It's no problem at all, I could hire some help. Help you tidy up a bit. Call a decent repairman and maid."

"No need," Dylan says. "I'm staying here for as long as it takes to sort things out."

"Wait, you are?" I ask. "Are you *sure*?"

"Yeah," Dylan says. "Want to make sure we finish what we started, right?" The word right rings differently. I know this means he's here to help me see this Oliver thing through, no matter the cost. What have I done right to deserve him? Or maybe we don't think we deserve anything but destruction and chaos.

"Right, right," I say. "*See*, I'm fine."

Auntie Lee clicks her tongue and replies, "Well, if you say so. But I am just a phone call away." She turns around to put her dish in the sink but drops it on the ground instead. The plate snaps in half, startling me.

"I, I need to go," she says. Something in her shifted.

An uneasiness spreads across her face. She mutters something about a shadow in daylight and makes the sign of the cross. Dylan and I exchange worried glances.

As Auntie Lee leaves the house, she misses a step on the front stairs, careening onto the brick walkway. Whether it was her rushing or something pushing her, I'll never know. But I know forearm bones aren't supposed to stick out of skin like a snapped no. 2 pencil. At least, the ambulance driver who came didn't seem to mind when she leaned her buffoon hair against his chest, wailing as they drove to the hospital. She regifted him the casserole.

We silently sit on the steps; long enough for the streetlamps to turn on and keep us company.

"You don't think…" Dylan trails off.

"Absolutely, I do."

He whistles. "Well, fuck."

"You know you don't have to stay here."

"Cara don't be an idiot. If I left now, after what just happened, what would you do?"

"But it's not your job –"

My work beeper buzzes. Before I can translate the numbers, Dylan snatches it out of my hands.

"Hey! Give that back. It could be an emergency."

"Cara, we're *in* an emergency, don't you get that?"

Of course, I get that. I just don't know where to start to fix this. Maybe I don't? Maybe I just live with this and do as much good as I can when I can. But I can't tell Dylan that. "I can handle this, you know?"

"No," he says. "You don't get to decide what's best for me. I don't care how much you try to push me away. I'm not budging. You've done *more* than enough. We don't have to talk about it, but I'm staying."

"Since when do you get sentimental?"

"Since when are you such an asshole? I don't have to be here. Don't forget that" he says, and hands me back my work beeper. He stares at me until I turn it off and shove it into my back pocket. "That's better."

A red sedan turns the corner and stops in front of the house. The driver sits inside for a bit. I know exactly what she's thinking: *Do I really want to get involved? Again? With her? After all this time of being ok?*

"Hey, who's that?" Dylan asks. "Wait, is that-"

"—Beth."

"Yep, that's my cue to go inside!"

"Wait, is that even safe? Dylan. Dylan! Oh, my fucking god..."

I yell after him but it's no use. He's already inside. By the time I turn around, she is standing in front of me. I've thought about this exact moment hundreds of times. Sometimes, I say nothing at all. I pull her as close to me as possible so I can feel her warm breath against my neck until I can't take it anymore and not kissing her feels like a thousand deaths. Other times, I hold her hand and deliver the sweetest soliloquy, admitting all that I had denied her and proposing all I will give. But when this moment actually arrives, when Beth looks up at me with her tawny eyes and a high ponytail that'd look stupid on anyone else in the world, all I can say is, "Oh."

"Hi, Cara," she says.

That alone is enough to make my heart stop.

"Why are you...?"

She snorts and shakes her head. "A 'hey' after no texts, no calls, no visits for a year. You don't think I know an 'I need your help' sign from you? After all this time? Now you're gonna invite me in or not?"

"Beth, I don't know if this is such a good idea."

"Hm, well, maybe you let me be the judge of what's right for me?"

"Why is everyone always telling me that?"

"Gee, I don't know, maybe because you have a pattern?"

"Well, I don't know about that..."

"I know your mother died, Cara," she says, putting a hand on my arm, sending flutters to my chest. I have no right to ask anything from Beth, but at this moment, I want everything from her. "The fact that you didn't think you could call to tell me," She shakes her head, "You don't have to go through this alone, ok?"

"No, well, yes, there's that but…You wouldn't have happened to bring your crystals?"

At the mention of crystals, Beth shoots me a confused look. "I'm sorry. Since when do you believe in my crystals? Wait, what did you and Dylan get into *now*?" That look I was all too familiar with fell across her face—the calculations, the trepidation, the knowingness of my messy orbit, and how it always pulls her into its hold.

I say the words she wants to hear and the ones I hate most, "I need your help."

***

If I hadn't, maybe I would have seen Beth again.

THOSE WHO DARE RETURN

Cara

"So, let me get this straight," Beth says. "After the cupboard, the washer machine, the nightmares, and Auntie Lee's broken arm, you all got drunk and decided to sleep it off in this house? That's your good idea?"

"Well, we were hungover for Auntie Lee," Dylan said, flopping on the couch. "So, you missed that."

"Is that tuna on your shirt?" Beth asks, so Dylan exaggeratedly licks it off. "Oh, men are so gross."

"Good to see you too, Beth," he says. "How's yogi life treating you?"

"I have an LLC now, so pretty damn good," Beth replies. "Also, I'm a life healer."

"Ha!"

"OK, cease-fire, you two," I say, pacing around the living room, unable to just sit fucking still.

To say Beth and Dylan don't get along is the biggest understatement in history. Growing up in our family, Dylan and I mastered the art of sarcasm, binge-drinking, and avoiding problems. Sometimes that's a beautiful thing. Other times, it means I use my rare free time for hangovers, and Dylan never gets the courage to finish his bachelor's degree in accounting so he can turn his landscaping gigs into a profitable small business. When Beth and I dated, I had a fridge of unasked-for green smoothies and lectures on Dylan's negative energy.

Beth's eyes dart around the room, stopping her gaze on the bed. "Is that…?"

"Yeah," I say. "Hospice hasn't picked it up yet."

"Huh," Beth says, biting her thumb as she thinks. "Where are these photos? The ones your mom kept in her armoire. Spirits don't come into a place without a connection. Maybe you missed something in them."

"Well, I burned one of them, but here." I push the manilla envelope toward her. "There's the rest of them. I haven't looked at them yet. I think, no matter how it sounds, that's what started all this."

"That doesn't make sense," Beth says. "You just told me the shadow man—"

"—Oliver," Dylan interjects.

"Fine, *Oliver*, he came *before* Dylan found this and before Dylan visited. Remember?"

God, she's so hot when she proves me wrong.

"You're right, yeah… I guess it all started the day of my mother's wake."

"Wait, hold up," Dylan says, getting up from the couch. "I thought you did card readings or some crap. What do you know about ghosts and 'connections?' Tell me, why should we listen to you, Gumby?"

"Dylan! Beth, I'm…"

"—I'm all you got," Beth says. "But to be honest, you should have found someone else. I do *tarot* readings and read auras. I don't have much spirit experience first-hand, just know what I've learned online."

"Oh, fucking fantastic," Dylan says. "The WebMD of ghost hunting. Cara, you hearing this?"

I swat Dylan in the arm. "Stop it."

"Give me *some* credit," Beth snaps. "I've *spoken* to people who've done seances and cleansings before. I just haven't done them myself. I know how but the practice of it, it can get rather messy. I need some time. I bet Mia would be online now—there's a whole Discord channel. What's your WiFi password? Same one?"

I put a hand on Beth's shoulder. "Hey, hey, are you sure? Look, I hear you, and I'm not doubting that you can, or that you want to, I get it, it's just… You *just* got here, and you're already in full gear. Aren't *you* always the one saying that we need to process where we're at before running ahead to what's next too fast?"

Beth puts her hand on my hand. Her lips twist as if she's holding back a smile. Our eyes meet and feel more like magnets, drawing us closer to one another. "Maybe you're right," she says. Of course, Dylan interrupts this before we can even call it a moment. He picks up one of the photographs and utters, "Oh, shit."

Sighing, I turn around and notice him lining up the pictures on the hospice bed. In total, there are four photos. "Look, look," he says, pointing at each one. "I didn't notice it before but they're all in a bed. I thought they were sitting but it's just the adjustable mattress pushed up, so it looks like that. Cara, they're all in bed."

"Yes, Dylan, that's what most elder care looks like."

"Ok, don't get cute just 'cause your girlfriend is around."

"We're not together," I say, doing my best to hide my blushing cheeks.

"Go on, Dylan," Beth quickly says, saving me from the embarrassment of it all. "What is it?"

"See, Gumby appreciates me," he says. "Look at the bed, Cara."

I walk closer to the photos, peering at each shot. At first, nothing stands out about them. Each photo is similar; an elderly person in their home, sitting up in bed, with my mother sitting in a chair beside them. Well, except for one photo. There's an elderly man in bed with a small boy hugging him with my mom smiling at them. But then I see it, the handrail lowered on the left side of the bed has a bend and deep scratch mark.

Oh, no.

When Susan dropped off my mom's hospice bed, she

apologized a thousand times, telling me about how the bedframe got stuck in one of the doorways at someone else's home, and they no longer make the replacement parts for it. "No," I say, shaking my head as if that'll make this all go away. "No, no, no, no."

Beth steps closer, peering at the photos from over my shoulder. "I don't…Oh."

"Nailed it!" Dylan says, doing a dance like Marcus Smart without any of his charisma.

"Oh my god, you haven't nailed anything yet," she hisses. "You just found out a part of why this is happening. We still have a *lot* to figure out here so take all that down a notch. Look at Cara, you idiot."

"Oh, shit… I'm sorry."

How did I get on the floor? I have no idea but I'm holding my knees and gently rocking myself back and forth as moonlight washes the room. The bed—it was so obvious. The odds? Infinitesimal. But hey, I've seen stranger things in our healthcare happen due to limited budgets and Rhode Island being so small you could watch a movie in the length of time it takes to travel our state. Mom died in the same bed as her patients. In a way, it'd be kind of perfect, if it didn't just stab me with the reminder of how she lived so much for them.

"Cara?" Beth asks, rubbing my back. "You ok?"

Dylan sits beside me. I notice the wet mark on my flannel shirt before I register I'm crying. Beth inches closer to me and rests her head on my shoulder, bringing me a small but needed jolt of peace. "When I was eight, I remember her calling me at home," I say. "She had picked up another shift and wouldn't be home until I was in bed. I was angry, so angry." I groan. "It wasn't a birthday. Or a holiday, though she worked those too. It was a Wednesday, an ordinary Wednesday. Somehow that made it worse. Like any day at all, if given the choice to be home or not, she wouldn't. I picked up this photo of us on the mantel and I smashed it." I use my sleeves to wipe my eyes dry and clear my throat. "I left it there for her to find it. But she never said a word to me."

The next day the glass shards were gone. I remember that the most. She never cared enough to ask why I did it or see if I had gotten cut or scraped in the process. Nothing like a cry for attention being ignored.

"When I did get to see her, I only saw the worst of her," I add. "Ugh, I don't even know why I'm talking about this now, of all times. But even in the end, it was only pain. Look, I've seen patients code before and flatline and that stuff's not new to me. I just remember standing here after her last inhale, waiting for that final exhale to come—maybe it'd give me some kind of relief to know that it was done, it was over, but… Now, fuck, it's all still here. Do you know what this means? If *they* are here, then somewhere, sometime, she is too."

I'm sobbing so hard that I don't know which pieces of this they heard. But I can feel their looks, god, how awful it feels. I can tell Dylan wants to say something, anything, but he has no idea what will help me feel better. Neither do I. And Beth, I am a puddle around her. I can feel myself spilling into her with abandon.

"Oh, Cara," Beth says. She pulls me close to her, so I can rest my head on her chest, letting the steady sound of her heartbeat work its calming and soothing magic. "Just let it out some, it's ok, just let it out of you."

I wipe my running nose, and though I don't want to, I stand up, putting space between us. "I'm fine," I say. "Just you get it, right? I don't care why this is happening, I just can't see her again. We need to stop it."

"Ok," Dylan says, heading straight toward the bed. "I'll bring it to the junkyard."

"Will that work?" I ask.

Beth sits with the idea for a second, mulling it over.

"Possibly," she says. "At the very least, how can it hurt to get rid of something that clearly is bringing up a lot for you? Wouldn't you want it to be gone?"

"Yes."

"That settles it," Dylan says, puffing out his chest. He's clearly happy to have something to do with his hands and that stops my crying. "I'll handle it, no matter what." Before we have time to weigh if it is a good idea or not for Dylan to take the bed alone, he's already hoisted it into the back of his pickup truck. He covers the dreaded thing with a bright blue tarp and ties it in securely. Beth and I watch him from inside the house.

After Dylan's car speeds away, Beth moves closer to me. I exhale, feeling relief at not having to stare at that fucking bed ever again. Her hand gently brushes up against mine. The sudden movement causes me to jump.

"Sorry," I say. "I'm a little on edge, I guess… I didn't mean to." I stumble for the right words to come.

"Of course, you're on edge," she says. "Who wouldn't be?"

"I *am* glad you're here, though."

"Maybe we should sit down?" Beth's eyes survey mine, looking for a spark. "Rest a little?"

When she says that, I know we're on a precipice. Whatever step I take next will alter everything we've spent a year building—the distance, the independence, the clear lines of where she and I begin and end. But Beth looks at me like she wants to cradle me in her arms until I surrender to the taste of her. How can I not?

The second we sit on the couch; I know we're undone—our clothes serve no purpose. Our mouths gasp for each other as if our kisses contain more oxygen than air. My hand slides down her naked back, tracing the slight tilt of her spine–scoliosis, the reason she got into yoga and healing aura stuff in the first place. She softly moans. I pull her closer. She can't be close enough. She'll never be close enough. My fingers trace the inside of her thighs, and she pulls me inside her. The start and end of her becomes the start and end of me.

***

This will be the last time we're ever this close. If only I knew that then, I'd have held her longer.

I rest my head on her breast, as our spindly legs intertwine on the couch. Her fingernails brush through my sweaty, tangled curls, massaging my scalp. Oh, the sweet release of it all. I nestle my head under the nook of her neck as if I could find shelter there. "Cara," she whispers, inspiring me to kiss the sides of her neck. "No, Cara," she repeats in a hushed tone. "Don't move. Just listen to me, do *not* move. We're not alone, here."

Beth is right.

I turn my head slightly and there isn't the black smoke I've come to fear. No, there is the wispy shape of an older woman in a nightgown. It's like she's made out of mist or fog—here and yet not here, all at once. Her image blips in and out of sight. With each blink, I think she's gone. But then, poof! She reemerges. She's small, with bones like a baby bird and pleading eyes. I should want to scream but something about her makes me sit up, despite Beth's attempts to pull me down and closer to her. "Cara, stop it," Beth says. "Just, don't."

But I don't think Beth sees what I see. The woman looks sad, not spiteful. Her lips are moving but I can't hear a word. I've seen this frailness before; the way cancer drains the bones and tissues of all shapes, fullness, and colors. What's left in all that thinning—all that want with nothing to hold it, that's her.

My heart aches for her, though I know that won't do her any good. As if she could feel that in me, she appears once more, brighter than before giving me a sense of warmth. A gust of wind blows my mom's photos onto the floor. One of them flips over, and it has the name Anna written on it. The spirit then disappears as if that act zapped her energy. I get up and turn over all the photos: *Oliver, Anna, Marie, Matthew & Lyle.*

"Anna," I say. But she doesn't reply. "Anna? Can you hear me?"

"Cara, what are you doing?!"

"You gotta believe me," I say. "I think she wants to help us. I feel it. I felt this calm. I can't really explain it, but it wasn't like with Oliver. That was just anger and hate. With her, it's just this… knowing sadness."

"How do you know it's not a trick?"

"Do you trust me?"

She holds my hand and replies, "I don't know how to answer that." When I pull back from her, Beth adds, "How can I, Cara? How can anyone do that in this situation? Who would I be if I just said sure, yeah?"

"No one asked you to *be* in this situation. You just showed up here."

"Oh, c'mon…What else was I supposed to do? Ignore you?"

With that, the sweetness of the air between us evaporated. We put on our clothes and found a new defense to name with each passing second. As more time passed, we became more convinced of each other's stubbornness. At least we agreed on staying in my bedroom, away from the living room, until Dylan returned.

***

I should have heard how her hesitation spoke volumes.

THE ONE WHO'S ALWAYS THERE

Dylan

As I drive on Route 37, I can't help but think about what a fucking mess we're in, and I got no idea if this will help. Of course, I lied to Cara! She needs to believe it'll work, or she won't get up from that floor anytime soon. I've seen it. See, Cara's too much in her own head. Trust me, I know this better than anyone. But that's what she has me for, someone to snap her out of that. Get her a pint. Take her mind off all the people she has or hasn't saved. She never forgets them. Like she has this running tally in her head of each patient. Who can live like that? Like *she* is the only thing standing between their life and death. Kinda self-absorbed, if you ask me, but I get it, her heart, it's aching to be in the right place—just overshoots. Beth *thinks* she can help her by diving into all that mess. But has that *healed* her? They talk and talk and talk and what has that done to help, huh?

Ugh, they're probably fucking right now. Let's see how long this go of it lasts. I give it three months. She turns Cara inside out and then who is left to deal with that? Ain't her. That'd be "crossing a boundary", but who draws these lines here, huh? Yeah, Cara is a mess, but Beth steamrolls in every time to fix her. Then, as soon as it gets *real*, as soon as the two of them have to sort their shit out, she bolts. Every. Single. Time.

Beth, no one, can give Cara what she wants most—a

mom who loved her unconditionally. With Auntie Laurie, there were always conditions. Cara thinks I don't remember, but I remember more than she does. I saw how she'd run around, mumbling about dinosaurs as a kid. All she wanted was for Laurie to smile and play with her. What'd she say? "Oh, that's nice." No eye contact. No pretending to be monsters. No hide-and-seek or lullabies. One Christmas, she gave her a vacuum cleaner toy as a gift, then told her how to unwrap presents in a way that's *cleaner*. There she was 6 years old, carefully folding tissue paper to store away like a maid.

Unbelievable. It only got worse as Cara got older and started speaking her mind. Some parents don't want children. They want an extension of themselves to control. I read that once in an *Oprah Book Club* pick. That's something. Cara will be ok, in time, but right now, she needs us to act like it. I have to act like it.

I pull into the junkyard on Huntington Avenue. I know a guy, Jimmy Savini Jr., so I don't have to call someone at 3 AM to open up the gates, I got keys. Helped him once get rid of a car without plates, and that's all I'll say on that one. I squeeze my truck into the open-ish lot, near some rusty grills, bent rims, and scatterings of hubcaps. Back in the day, Cara and I used to steal hubcaps from junkers and whatnot before all the plastic models came out and ruined the bit. Never made much, but ay, we were never caught, so I call it a win-win.

After shifting some equipment around in the back, I haul the mattress out of the cargo bed. Doesn't weigh much, something shy of 200 lbs., I bet. That's a leg day for me. The bed thumps on the ground, bringing with it a cloud of dirt that goes right up my nose. I sneeze and wipe my face with the back of my sleeves.

When the dusting clears, it hits me. Eventually, someone will come looking for this. Might be the time to call in some favors but at least it's outta the house. At least, Cara has one less thing to sort through now.

I give her a lot of shit, but she's all the family I have left. The one who'll always pick up my call and that's a rare thing. My mom used to say if you can count on one hand friends like that, you live a charmed life. Doesn't mean that comes easy. But it means when it gets rough, you show up. You never, ever back down.

Back in the truck, the radio station ain't nothing but static. No matter what channel I go to, all I hear is a crinkling sound. Figures. I pop in an old cassette tape and hum along to "We've Only Just Begun," which I'll only do when no one else is driving with me. I like that Karen. She soothes me. Hands down better drummer than Collins and Grohl combined. As I turn onto the highway, the chorus gets stuck in a loop—*We've only just, we've only just, we've only just, we've only just.* "What the...?" I slam the dash and the skipping stops.

They don't make cassettes like these anymore and I don't want to pay $300 on eBay for one. Besides, this one is special. This one my mom gave me on my seventh birthday. The skipping resumes, *We've only just, we've only just, we've only just.* Goddamnit. I push the volume knob off and eject the tape to save it. A couple of seconds later, the radio sings *begun, begun, begun.* Oh, fuck me. Oh, fuck. There's not even a tape inside!

The temperature drops inside the truck as if I got shoved into a walk-in freezer.

When the evening comes, we smile...

Nope, nope, nope. Fuck this car, fuck this day.

I push my foot onto the pedal. Faster, and faster, I drive back to Cara. If this shit is starting up here, now, there's no way to know what's happening to her back home. I gotta be there for her if it gets rough.

The windshield wipers turn on, smudging the windshield with dirty streaks. I grip the wheel tighter, doing my best to stay steady, stay calm–inhale, exhale, inhale, exhale—as it gets harder and harder to see. Worst thing you can do is jolt a wheel left or right on the road, gotta stay in the middle, hands at 9 and 3 o'clock. The wheel is shaking but I'm holding firm, clenching my fists tighter until my knuckles are white as bone.

Takin' it over, just the two of us...

Dawn hasn't quite broken through the sky, but there are enough drivers on the road to make my stomach drop. Just steady. The windshield wipers increase in speed. The volume nob goes on full blast.

Focus, Dylan. You got this.

We'll find a place where there's room to grow...Together, together, together...

"Stop fucking with Karen!" I shout to the car.

The steering wheel jerks to the left, though I'm using all my strength to keep it center. Think about Cara. Think about how she needs you, how you need her, how she never gives you a boring day in your life, pal. *Keep center.* An 18-wheeler truck pulls up on my left and its heft and speed suction my truck closer to its metallic underbelly. I try to steer right and center but the wheel shifts, sending me right toward its back wheel. Fuck, fuck, fuck, fuck. The truck blares its horn as if screaming for me to stop. Trust me, buddy, I want to! More than anything. I try. But I can't. I'm sorry, Cara. I'm so sorry. I exhale, closing my eyes to what will be.

When I open my eyes, the windshield is clean and there is no trucker beside me. I'm parked in front of Cara's mom's house. Huh. This wasn't about trying to kill me. Just wanted to tease what it *could* do if I left the house. Robins chirp away as the sun rises in the sky. Before I even get inside the house, I know what I'll find.

Am I right? You better believe it. Somehow, the bed is still there. Cara and Beth are in Cara's old bedroom, going back and forth about something. I can't hear what, but I can tell they're not on the same page by their volume. Shocker! In the living room, I rub my eyes, but it's still fucking there. That.

Damn. Bed. As much I hate to say it, we're gonna need some of Beth's woo-hoo.

"How is this even possible?" I say to it as if it'll reply back. I kick its metal legs and shove it. If I can't beat it, I sure as hell am not gonna let it win without a fight.

What the fuck did we do, huh? What did Cara do? With each thought, I punch the mattress. Again, again, again. Fuck. This. Thing.

"What are you doing?" Beth asks.

I turn to see Beth and Cara staring at me with alarmed looks on their face.

"Dylan, why is the bed back here?" Cara asks. "What the hell happened?"

"God, what did you do, now?"

"I didn't," I try to say, but wave my hands at them. "Forget it. It just didn't work. Ok? It just didn't fucking work and I don't know what to do." I punch it again, and again, and on the third time, the bed jolts. The whole frame comes flying at me, knocking me over with ease. My head slams against the tile floor. Blackness clouds my vision. "Cara," I say. "We've only just..." I hear my words as I slip into the enveloping darkness. But I know they don't make much sense to her. I didn't have enough time to tell her more. I would have, I would, I...

***

Cara

"Dylan!" I scream. "Beth, quick get me some towels."

"God, that's so much blood," she says, swaying. She's not someone that does well with the sight of blood. But I can't have her fainting too. "What, what do we do? I didn't. I said to him, but I didn't mean..."

"Don't look," I say. "Bathroom, now, towels. Go!"

She brings me the towels, as blood pools underneath

Dylan's head—a deep, dark blossoming red. I try to stay calm. Head wounds bleed *a lot*. They don't always mean what they look like they mean. This could be four or so stitches and aspirin bad. I go to apply direct pressure to the head wound, but then I see the cracked scalp, the exposed fleshy brain. Oh, fuck. He's gonna need antibiotics and a heck of a lot more than I have here.

"Dylan, Dylan, can you hear me? Can you blink?"

"What do I..."

"Call 911, Beth, he's not responding. Now!"

"I'm going to be sick... Ok, ok, I'm calling."

Oh, Dylan. I want to cradle him tight, but I know I can't move him much, that'll just make it worse. A familiar coppery smell invades my nostrils. "Stay with me, Dylan," I beg. My hands are shaking. My voice cracks. "Please, please, don't leave. You promised to see this through." I feel his pulse, it's there but weak, drifting away.

Tears fall against his cheeks but they're not his. He can't cry right now, only I can. I'm not sure how long I sit there, holding his wrist and counting. Eventually, Beth tells me the medics are here. The two men have to pry my hands off Dylan to take him away. Minutes after they leave, I'm still holding the blood-stained towels.

"They said they'll call us back with news," Beth says, breaking the silence between us. I furiously scrub the floor, as Beth does her best to look away from the red soapy foam. "We just have to wait."

"I should be there, at the hospital. What if they apply too much pressure and rupture a blood vessel? Or Dylan, the dumbass he is, tries to get up from his bed? They don't have enough staff for his stubbornness..."

Beth sighs, biting her lip. Clearly, she wants to say something but is holding back. "What?"

"What do you think *you* can do there that other nurses and doctors can't? I understand that you want to make sure things go the right way but c'mon, Cara, just have some faith in the universe, ok?"

"Fuck the universe." I grab my coat, but Beth blocks my way from the front door.

"Cara, breathe, just take a second to let this all sit in, ok? We don't even know why Dylan came back or the bed. I think some of this might be out of our hands. I get that's scary, but you saw what happened."

She's not wrong. I've never seen a bed fly across a room like a bullet. How could I stop that?

"I have to do something, Beth."

"I know, I know. But... You saw what happened. I don't think we can just leave anymore. We don't know what more damage that might cause us or Dylan. We can't risk that."

"How do you know that for sure? I've left the house before."

"I don't," Beth says. "But I know cause and effect. We saw Dylan leave with the bed and try to get rid of it and look what happened to him. Besides *you have* been having nightmares, it's not like whatever it is hasn't been messing with you this whole time. I just... I think we're on a new level here, and we need to be careful."

"Ok, then we need to talk to Anna."

"Cara..." she says, then takes a deep exhale. "Do you really think she'll help us?"

"Yes, I do. You don't have to trust me, but just give me this. Besides, if we're already fucked, what harm could it do to at least *attempt* to save ourselves. We already let Dylan down. I let him take that bed."

"Ok, ok, we'll give it a shot. But don't say I didn't warn you."

After I finish cleaning up the floor, Beth gathers some candles and salt. She lights the wicks and hums softly, settling her mind. She makes a summoning circle on the ground for us to call upon Anna, with a ring of salt surrounding us. She says that it'll protect us from outside forces, though she doesn't answer me when I ask about inside ones. We sit on the floor, holding hands as loosely as possible. Tension pulsates between us.

What we didn't know then was that Anna wouldn't talk to us. But someone else would, and she made all the difference.

THE ONE WHO ANSWERED

Beth

I would never in a thousand years admit this, but Cara's right. I didn't *have* to come here. As I trace lines of salt onto the floor, I know I shouldn't be here with her. Why did I come? *Why* do I always find myself back here, even though I know it won't work? I've asked myself this countless times. No answer makes enough sense. Sometimes, we get into these relationships that hold this power on us, like a knee-jerk reflex, we move for them. Their grip digs deep into our central nervous system, overriding every thought, every matter.

She's mine, the unsolvable problem. I always believe *this* time; I'll figure us out.

In some ways, seances are simpler than us. It's all about the summoning, the pulling them toward you until the lines between the two of you blur. You're a vessel for them to speak through, a tether to reality. Spirits arrive because they're called. They don't have to like or want it. They just follow the ask. At least with this, I'm the one doing the calling. For once, I'm not the one who feels beckoned to her, to impossibly be her everything.

Cara keeps trying to lock eyes with me, but I don't want to maintain eye contact. The longer I look into her eyes—blue shards of sea glass with flecks of hazel—I lose more of my will to leave, and I know I have to go.

"Almost done?" Cara asks.

"One second," I say, even though I am ready, just stalling for time.

I know I'll have to leave. I know leaving her is the only thing that'll keep me on the right track, not forgetting appointments with my clients, not foregoing my breath work and yoga classes, not breaking social plans because I want to fuck her until I'm brainless. When I'm with her, I let everyone in my life down.

Being with her, she's all I think about. It's suffocating. At first I love the nosedive, a chance to let go, to give into a version of me who forgets worrisome things like follower counts or having the best headstand. With her, enough is enough. Until it's not. Even now, here, I feel myself becoming consumed doing something I'd never do otherwise. I blame Laurie for most of our issues. If Cara succeeded at something and told her, she was arrogant and self-centered. If she failed, she deserved it. Not to mention, well, the parts Cara only tells me when she's high out of her mind or drunk after hanging with Dylan. Still, Cara always showed up to help her–translating bank statements into common sense or writing her resumes, her hospice care was no different. But all that fixing, it took her further and further away from keeping herself and *her* life together. The first— of many—times that we dated; I try to get Cara to empathize with Laurie. I wanted her to see that hurt people hurt people and if she could lead with compassion then they'd be ok.

Cara just silently nodded, looking at me with this knowing melancholy. I didn't get it then, that look of devastating hopelessness. I wanted to make them work. The first time we visited Laurie for Thanksgiving—based on my request—a disagreement about salad escalated into locking ourselves into Cara's bedroom until Laurie screamed herself tired. Holidays brought out the worst of it, but the most chilling thing was how calm Cara was, how ordinary and expected this was; the blood-curdling shouting, whacking against her door with balled fists holding a lifetime of regret in need of pushing it all onto Cara. Eventually, she did calm down.

The next day, Laurie pretended nothing happened. Cara did the dishes. In the car ride home, I'll never forget what she said, "This is why I have the rule that we don't do nights there. But you wanted to try it, so we did. You didn't understand. Now you've felt an ounce of it, can you imagine how it feels to still love her?"

When I heard Laurie died, I worried. I didn't know how Cara could function without needing to be needed by her. At times, she cut off ties with her mother, but Cara, deep down, wanted to believe things could change. But they never did. How do I make that pain go away? I can't but I want to support her somehow. Look where that got me—a friggen seance. She makes me lose my mind. Still, I wouldn't trust anyone else to help her.

The living room has these big windows, so Cara calls it a sunroom because it's full of light during the day. But at night here, there's nothing but shards of moonlight and the creak of the house settling. We sit in the center of the room and half of Cara's face is draped in shadow. If the heat was on, it didn't feel like it. When I exhale, I see the cloud of my breath. That chill sent shivers down my body.

Someone is coming.

"Ok," I say and close my eyes. "Anna, if you're still here, we're listening."

"Am I supposed to say anything?"

"No, not yet, and stop fidgeting. I need to focus."

"Ok, ok, just checking."

I roll my neck and shoulders, loosening my muscles. My fingers are so cold I can barely feel them. That chillness spreads up my wrist to my forearm, then my elbow, branching out into each vein and pore of my body.

"Ok, take two. Anna…Anna, do you hear us?"

In the middle of the circle, her photo lies face-down. I open my eyes and watch the picture tilt, ever so slightly, as if mustering up the strength to flip itself over. "Anna, we're listening. What do you want to say?" I ask and the photo tilts even more. I ignore Cara's questions for now because I have to focus on the feeling—I am a vessel tied to a rope and outreaching the ends of me to her, to grasp onto, and pull. Exhaling, I imagine her fingers tentatively touching mine, sliding her fingers closer until our hands are threaded together as one.

The photo flips over. "Holy shit," Cara says.

I am the vessel. I am the vessel. I am the vessel. Take the rope. Take the rope. Take the rope.

"Anna?" I call out. The candles around us flicker, crackling.

Inhale. Exhale. Inhale—oh, there it is. The cinching of us. The sound of a key twisted into the proper lock. I'm here but I'm of two minds—hers is in front and I am the whisper behind it, the shadow to her light.

"I'm not Anna," we say.

"Then... Who are you?" Cara asks us, with a trembling voice. We imagine the three other photos in the center of the circle. Here they come, fluttering over. There, that's good. We need them. We need to show Cara the others. We need to explain before he comes: The Terror.

We pick up one of the photos and point at it, saying, "Her." It's been a while since we knew of things like names—the longer you're dead, how easy it is to forget those titles that don't amount to much in the end. But we feel a familiar pang when we see the letters on the back of the photo. Ah, that's right. "Marie," we say.

"Ok... Marie, um, where is Anna? She came to me, and I want to speak with her."

"No."

"No?"

"No, she's too weak. Not as weak as Oliver, that puff of smoke, but almost there. She'll get there in time, we all do. She's resting, gathering herself. We can speak with you, though, and you should listen, Cara."

"Wait, we? Who else is there?"

"Beth is still here, of course. That's how I have her voice. She's lending it to me."

"Is Beth ok? Beth?"

"She's fine, but now we'll tell you a story about your mother."

"Wait, what does..."

"Didn't she teach you never to interrupt someone."

The candles in the room extinguish. We did that. We make the moonlight disappear too, placing us in the darkest of darkness. No distractions here. This place of no place. This room of no room. We speak.

Greenwood Estates wasn't the fanciest of nursing homes, but it was ours. Mine, Oliver's, Anna's, and Matthew's. There was always a warm meal that we never had to cook and always something to busy ourselves with like a field trip to the zoo or watching some high schoolers flatly play a trumpet. Little comforts and close quarters. We came to the facility at differing times for differing reasons, but we rather enjoyed each other's company. Anna loved to play Gin Rummy, though she never tallied the scores right. I let her win because of her condition. Oh, that's not rude of me to say, we all had something wrong with the nuts and bolts of us. For her, it was brain cancer. Sometimes we'd be in the sitting room watching Columbo and she'd think I was her daughter, even though she was only five years older than me. Other times, she'd become obsessed with the idea that one of us was stealing her pudding. I had hemophilia so Oliver and Matthew helped me with most things like hallways, which can be a bugger, every doorway becomes a possible disaster with my bags of bones. Oliver had a stroke, so he relied on a cane and us to help him with writing or holding certain objects as his whole left side wasn't much use to him. And Matthew, well, he was just old. Too old to live by himself as he got forgetful sometimes too. He had a son named Lyle, someone he fostered in his later years, the darling he was—and he was afraid of being a burden to him. The little one would visit us too and secretly bring us chocolate bars slightly melted so we could chew them up deliciously.

Guess what all of us also had in common? Your mother.

She was our attending nurse and when each of us died, she was by our side. I think Oliver had a bit of a crush on your mother, despite him being twenty years her senior. Barely had any hair left but he'd spend hours combing it over to one side and putting on far too much aftershave before she visited him. But after a while, Oliver grew weak. They said it was an infection and some complications made it hard for him to breathe.

Your mother, well, she took pity on him. Oliver asked for a favor. Can you guess what it was? Smart cookie like you probably already figured it out. He asked to die by her hand, an act of mercy, he called it. We all couldn't argue with him. Once he made up his mind, that was that.

So she did what was asked of her, and that's where that nasty habit began. Making the pain stop is what she told herself she wanted for him, for others. A quicker way to find them some sweet relief, to stop the needless struggling. A little extra morphine here or there in moaning mouths, the medicine went down, down, down.

Some of us didn't want to go down though, no, we wanted to stay. Oliver and Anna, they said yes. But the rest of us, we wanted a little more time in the spring sunlight, hearing the crushed sounds of leaves in autumn, smelling the cinnamon spirit of the holidays, and being too old to fret about our bodies in swimsuits. I wanted that.

I don't much care for anger nor does Anna. We drift. We remember and we forget. Drifting between what was and is and eventually we'll become smoke and then become fog and then tiny particles that drift and drift—forgetting what form was, what was was, what what. But Cara, the others aren't too happy right now.

I'll do my best to keep them calm, quiet, stop with all this fussing and hurting. Oliver is just trying to protect your mother, her memory, this house, but Matthew and The Terror, well, you will have to face them.

Goodnight for now, darling.

Moonlight returns to the room as if someone yanked a blanket off all the windows. The candles are lit. Their thin warm flames sway side to side, casting dancing shadows onto the tile floor. I am back. Here.

I gasp, feeling as if I've emerged from being held deep, deep underwater. Marie is gone. My head throbs and I feel woozy. Cara grabs me and I lean into her. Everything is so cold, and I can't help shaking.

"Beth, Beth, are you ok?!" Cara screams.

I look up at Cara and pull her head toward mine. I kiss her deeply, savoring the taste of her tongue on mine—that warmth, that realness. "Yes," I say, clinging tighter to her and slightly shivering from all of it.

"Do you, do you remember what happened?"

I nod. "Yes, I was there, just not in the driver's seat so to speak. Cara, I'm sorry. I can't."

"You can't what?"

"Your mother, I, I'm sorry you had to find out that way…"

"Shh," she says, rocking me. "Don't worry right now, just rest."

I can tell the news weighs on Cara's mind, but she won't admit it to me, not yet. Her eyes are a thousand miles away. They get like that sometimes, as if something inside her clicks off and she's here but also elsewhere.

"But I—"

"Oh shit, Beth, your nose," she says. "It's bleeding. Let me get you something for that. Just pinch it and hold your head down, not up like all the dummies say. You want to make sure the blood drains out of you."

I touch my nose and red droplets fall on my hand. The wooziness returns without Cara there to steady me. Thankfully, I'm already sitting on the floor so when I pass out, there's not much more than a dull thud.

***

I've had a lot of time to think here, to replay and replay what happened. Eventually, it'll feel enough, and I'll open that door. But not yet… not yet.

WHAT WE HAVE TO LOSE

Cara

When I return to the living room, Beth is curled into a ball on the floor. Aw, fuck. I run over and check her pulse, a steady, thuh-thumb, thuh-thumb. Good. Ok, ok, she's alive. For a second, I hear the sound of my mother's last breath, I was there when it happened. When she went from a person to the most chilling of phrases—a body. I place my head on Beth's chest, comforted by the sound of her being. I probably shouldn't have asked Beth to do this, but she said she wanted to help, right? I didn't force her to come here and what other options do we have? Maybe she just needs to rest. Beth mumbles something too low for me to hear.

"Beth, you ok?"

"I think so? I'm just… tired."

"Ok, ok, you rest. I'll be right here."

I gently clean her face with a soft towel and carry her to the couch. She's shivering, so I drape a fuzzy blanket over her and crank the heat so high I start to sweat. I keep my head on her chest, *thu, thumb, thu thumb*, as if my presence is keeping her breathing. I wish I had that power, that I could inflate her when needed.

I stare at the bloody face cloth. Beth hates the sight of blood, the smallest of things but would always lead to us fighting when I'd forget and have *Friday the 13th* on at max volume. Even the description of blood sends her stomach reeling, which made it super hard to talk about any of my ICU shifts. I'd have to present my day in the vaguest of ways "a car crash with casualties" or "kitchen cooking incident." I didn't get it. She said it made her feel too much and told me something about empathy and mirror neurons in the brain. The memory makes me smile, despite, well, everything. I'm amazed she kept it together as well as she did when Dylan fell. Maybe the adrenaline helped. Oh, Dylan. God, it's all my fault. I can't undo any of this. What have I done?

Maybe Marie will help us. Maybe that's something? I need to believe in something. In all this loss and losing, I need a sliver of hope, some sort of promise that will last longer than me, keeping Beth and Dylan safe.

I blow out the candles and sit beside Beth in the dark. I can't tell if it's dawn or dusk or some muddied time in between. All of this feels like one unending, exhausting day. All I want to do is collapse. So, I do.

Something stirs, jolting my eyes open. The room is dark. The bed is still on the other side of the room. If it had moved, it stopped when my eyes opened. What's it waiting for? Maybe this is the point of it? Just make me worry and worry until I forget about worrying and feel calm and then it'll strike? Sadistic motherfucker.

There's a level of sleeplessness that makes surrender feel sweet. I'm there. Besides, I can't leave Beth. I need to hear her inhale and exhale, I need to know that she is still okay, and I didn't really hurt her, this time.

I settle back into cuddling Beth. Minutes later, I hear the sound of a zipper. My eyes flash to the bed. No one is near the thing. No smoke. No glimmer of Anne. But when I squint, I see a rustling, almost as if a mouse is inside the mattress, shuffling around under the covers. I lean closer in, trying to make shapes out in the dark. There's something there, in the open seam, a pearly white oval poking through the mattress' cover.

What the fuck?

Whatever it is, stops moving when I look directly at it. I turn my head away slightly, so I can just make out the image in the corner of my eye.

The whiteness takes an oval shape, sliding outward. Now it's longer and thinner.

A finger, poking through, curling upward.

Another finger emerges, and another, and another—reaching, reaching until its pale, wrinkled hand sticks out of the mattress seams. A second-hand breaks through and both of them pull and pull the covering open wider, wider, until two chalky arms sprout out into the suffocating darkness. *Cara, Cara...* the voice says as its shoulders peak through the sheets. Its cowered head rises up, up, up. I can't see its face, but I can't look away. Something holds me there, watching. Muscles have lost their meaning. My tongue is a slab of dead flesh.

A pale foot steps onto the floor. The toenails are gnarled and twisted like decaying tree branches. A step and then another and then, the waiting. It wants me to look at it. But I know once I do, I know I will be all over.

Still, it stands. It, unlike me, has all the time in the world.

"Cara?" Beth asks, shaking me awake. "Cara, your phone is ringing."

"Ok, ok," I say. "Just give me a second. I had a fucked-up dream."

"You ok?"

"Not in the slightest."

I blearily answer my phone. The call is from Kent Hospital and it's about Dylan's condition. I leap off the couch and ask a million questions. They say he's stable and talking and no memory loss apparent. But he has to stay on bed rest for a bit due to his head injury. No sudden stress or strenuous activity. He's on a course of antibiotics too, so no drinking and plenty of rest.

"Dylan asked to stay with you," the doctor says. "We can't legally force him to stay here, but it's up to you, if you think it's a good environment for him to recover."

My stomach drops.

"What is it?" Beth asks. "What are they saying?"

I could have said no, right then and there. But I'd be lying to myself if I said I ever considered an alternative.

***

"Of course, he can stay with us," I say. "We'll come pick him up soon."

After I hang up the phone, I turn to face Beth. I felt her daggers before I saw the look in her eye, boiling lava readied to erupt. "How could you say yes," Beth said. "We *just* talked about how it's not safe to leave without knowing the consequences of that bed. Jesus, Cara, you just change your mind like that?"

"What am I supposed to do? Let Dylan rest with a head injury at his house? Alone? You can't let someone do that what if he slips into a coma! Or he drinks on his meds. Someone needs to look after him."

"Oh, is that it?"

"Yes. Why are you so angry all of a sudden?"

Beth throws the blanket off the couch and starts putting on her socks and shoes. "Oh, don't do that, not now. You never change, do you? This isn't about Dylan's safety, and you know that. You just *want* to see him, didn't even ask me if it was ok. Didn't even think that you leaving to get him could put me in danger?"

"We'd go together, right? Safety in numbers? Wait... Where are you going?"

"Cara, I just became a freaking VESSEL for you, and you haven't even asked me if I'm ok. If you're going to endanger me anyway then I might as well just go... not like you'll make it any better in the long run."

"I just woke up, and I did ask, last night, I did!"

"Did you even once think about the risk of me doing it? Honestly?"

"I... I just wanted answers."

"Ugh! You don't see it, do you? Your mother, Dylan, and ghosts, you can't stand to help yourself. You say your life is a mess because you're busy helping everyone else, but that's just to fill that impossible hole in you. People like me and Dylan then swoop in to deal with your messes because you assume we always will."

That did it. The final twist of the knife to what was left of my heart. Kindness has left the building. My body becomes a steel trap, impervious and unfeeling. All the warmth I felt towards Beth hours ago fades far, far away. The part of myself that I hate most is this one—a trapdoor like trigger of my central nervous system I can't control. No breaching through that armored cage. Once it drops, I am the coldest version of humanity.

Beth looks away from me. "I know I'm supposed to say that I took it one step too far, but I'm not, Cara. You have and you do, and you will push and I'm just so tired of this crap. I care about you, and I hope that you'll take care of yourself but if I stay, I just make it worse. I give you an excuse to be a complete mess."

I say nothing. Give her nothing—no remorse nor hope.

Despite the tone of her voice, her eyes well up with tears.

"Fine," Beth says. "This is where I draw the line. If we can't be on the same page, now, of all times when our *lives* are on the line, I can't do this with you, any of it. I tried. I really tried, Cara. I love you."

"Sorry, I'm too broken for you," I say, knowing it'll hurt her. But like she says, hurt people hurt people, and she's leaving at the worst moment of my life when there are fucking *ghosts* out to kill me. What a choice.

Before Beth can snap back, the doorbell rings. The

sound quiets our fight for now, as curiosity gets the better of us. I answer the door and a 60-something year old man with a faded Red Sox baseball cap on smiles at me. "Hi, I'm just checking in to see if you and your family need anything," he says. "I used to go for walks with Laurie around the neighborhood. I couldn't make it to the services. Felt awful about not showing up sooner."

"I'm sorry, who are you?" I ask.

"Oh, apologies, I'm Larry. The one with the fuzzy terrier your mom likes so much."

Before my mom went on hospice, we were under one of our estranged times. I hadn't seen her in almost two years. The few calls we had were cordial and brief, cheery and as informative as a grocery list. I had never heard of Larry, but I know my mother liked to take walks around the neighborhood and chat with everyone.

"Larry, appreciate you dropping by, but not a good time," I snap.

I go to close the door, but Larry's hand stops me. "Oh, I'm sorry to hear that," he says.

"Yes, yes we're all sorry," Beth says. "Did you know Laurie well?"

I shoot a look at Beth. "We'll see you later."

"When?" Larry asks, which twists my guts into knots. His gaze never leaves my face and he's standing much, much too close to me. His breath smells of coffee rinds and cough drops. I shouldn't be able to smell him.

"Next week," I lie.

"What day, sugar?"

"Next Monday," I nearly spit out the word.

Larry nods, "What time?" His tongue rubs against the front of his yellowed teeth.

Whenever time I'm not fucking home, Larry. Take a fucking clue.

"7:00 PM," I say.

"Ok, sounds like a date." He winks, which makes me wince. "I'll be seeing you soon."

I lock the front door and watch Larry walk away until he's out of vision. What a creep. "Ok, Beth," I begin to say but when I turn around, Larry is inside my house. That, now that's enough to blast that steel-trap around my heart to fucking bits. He's holding Beth from behind, squeezing her and covering her mouth with his bony hand with a greasy smirk on his shriveled face. He clicks his tongue and says, "No manners, the kids these days. What a shame. Oh, don't worry about Beth. She's going to have a gas of a time with me."

"How the fuck?!"

He chuckles, exposing a rotted tooth on his bottom jaw. "I guess we haven't really had proper introductions. How rude of me. Guess it's contagious," he laughs. "Well, let's fix that, shall we?"

"Don't hurt her, ok? Please. What do you want?"

Again with that *click, click, click* of his tongue. "You know, where would the fun be? Skipping right to it? No, dear ol' Beth here, I'll send her someplace to wait for me to play with her, and play, I will, hehehe."

"What are you talking about, Larry?"

"I'll show you the Play-Pen soon enough, but for now…" Larry lets Beth go and I lunge forward to grab her tight. My fingers bristle up against her arm but then he claps his hands twice, and she's gone. "Bye-bye, Beth, hehehe. We need to have some conversations. You and I, we do. I believe you've heard of me. I'm Matthew."

I go to speak, but I have no lips. I. Have. No. Lips?! My fingers rub the area where my mouth used to be but find only smooth flesh. My tongue presses up against a wall of tissue, it can't escape. I gulp for air.

"Shh, there's a time to listen, and that time is now. Breathe through your nose, sugar. Tried to get your attention last night but you are the type who needs stronger methods to pay attention to anyone but yourself. Pity, that is. Marie and Anne are taking an ethereal nap of sorts so let's make the most of our time together."

He claps his hands twice. The floors, the walls, and the rooms around me disappear. I'm falling and falling into nothingness. No space. No voice.

Eventually, I land in Room 322 at Greenwood Estates. I can't see Matthew, but I hear him like a voiceover narrating his world to me. *Memory walking, it's a trip, ain't it, hehehe? Just wait and see, Cara.*

Witnessing what's to come is all I have the power to do.

WHO SHE USED TO BE

Cara

No matter how hard I push my tongue against where my lips used to be, it can't break the fleshy barrier. I can't open my mouth to ask where he took Beth, or why he's taking me here instead of where she is.

Now, now, sugar. Don't try to talk. Just settle in, look around. I bet you never felt like this, huh? How strong an urge it is, how primal the want, the need to speak. But you can't, can you? You can't utter a single word, but your mind reaches for it— the tippiest, toppiest shelf, oh, you can almost grasp that syllable, that curve of tongue.

And yet, nothing. Nothing but a scream turned inside out— all hollowed-like. That's you.

Matthew clicks his tongue again and again; the sound feels like someone flicking my ear. I'm in a room, his room, I'm guessing. The sunflower curtains are pulled back so he can look out from his bed at the greenery below. The crochet matches, the walkers slowly perusing across sidewalks, a parade of gaudy sunhats.

I look at my hands and jump backward in surprise. They're old and shriveled as prunes.

Oh, hush, don't be so dramatic. I don't look that bad, darling.

I'm in his head. I am *him*. An old white male. This is how I die? Of all the ways? Jesus Christ...

As I was so generously explaining, it's hard to want a thing you know won't ever come. Or that you had it and well, it won't come back again. Sorta like you and that Beth there, oh, don't look so cross. She'll be fine, enough… But what you're feeling, that pent-up razzled nature of yours, that was my day, my every day for years.

I could see everything, hear everything, but those words? Oh, at first, I could see them in my head but then it just all blurred, a fog so thick and dark I couldn't see through it after a point. I knew I had something to say but how? How became an unsolvable mystery, I became a mystery to myself. Words abandoned me too in the end.

Bet you never once thought about how it'd feel to get old, how some of us get locked inside our own bodies and you just see the shell of us as we squirm and wither away on the inside looking out? Well, feel it, sugar.

Well, fuck, now I'm starting to feel bad for the creep. What the fuck is wrong with me?

Good, good, settle in a bit. You see, I got something to show you, something you'd never expect.

The room shifts around me like I'm on a tilt-a-whirl. Room 322 becomes a lounge. Soon I recognize Marie, Anne, and Oliver sitting down at a table with a deck of cards. They're younger than in their photos, not by much but less worn around the eyes, fuller hair, and none of them look pale or on IV-only diets. Oliver has a big mole on the side of his bald head that looks like the shape of Idaho, he keeps scratching it though Marie swats his arm each time. Anne looks up at me from behind thick-rimmed glasses attached to a necklace of glittery beads that shimmer in a room so beige, so full of dull paintings of fruit still-life or seagulls atop old whaling ships. She waves at me to hurry up and sit down as if a show is about to start and I'm running late.

Go on, don't be shy. It'll happen anyway but it's easier if you don't try to resist. Choice is yours, darling. I'll have my fun either way. But aren't you a bit itching curious to know what we all were like in the before times?

He's not wrong, so I sit down with the trio. Marie places her hand on mine and says, "I'm so glad you came, Matthew. I know you're all upset that Lyle couldn't be here. But there's always next Wednesday."

Oliver takes a handful of cashews out of his pockets and starts crunching into them one by one, adding, "Summer camp is only one week. Let the boy have some fun. We sure as hell ain't going nowhere. Cashew?"

I've always been allergic to cashews. Not like Oliver was the type to remember a damn thing.

Anne hushes the group as other residents file into the room. Orderlies bring in some extra chairs, and it looks like some sort of performance is about to happen. They even move the room's television out of the way, replacing it with two chairs. "They better have brought new songs this time," Anne says. "I'm missing Murder, She Wrote," to which Marie replies, "Oh, hush. The husband is the killer and I saved you an hour of life. Now, quiet! She's coming!" Anne huffs but I can see a smirk she's trying to hide. Marie, always the savior, huh?

Of all of us, Marie always cared the most about everybody. See, she somehow had that gift for knowing just what to say and how with such bright dimples and finesse and it worked. All gosh darn time, it worked. But she never had to go through any big heartbreak to get there. Not like people like us, Cara, who get gutted something fierce so, well, we know just how to hurt someone and when someone is hurting. But we don't act like Marie, now, do we?

When the duo emerges, my heart beats so fast in my chest that I think it might explode. In this version of an elder home stage, I saw Dylan's mom, Sally, with her rosewood-colored Gibson guitar. Beside her, my mom is in scrubs but with more makeup than she used to wear, and her hair done up nicely too and *smiling*. That right there was almost enough to destroy me. I don't remember the last time I saw her genuinely smile. When she came home from work shifts, I heard the sob stories, her anger at mortality and illness. Each time someone died, it was like this ripple effect where she'd bemoan each loss again and again—that's what she gave me. As I lived, as I grew and changed shapes and directions—that part of life, my precious life, was utterly unimportant to her. I don't think she'd remember a single name of my ex-girlfriends, but she remembered *every* patient and their death.

What a surprise! Did you guess it? Did ya, hehehe?

I try to leave but a pair of invisible hands press down on my shoulders, digging nails into my skin. Sharp pain shoots down my arms, as if Matthew's crusty fingernail spliced a nerve or two in halves and thirds. I look up and down my arms but there is no sight of blood. No one else seems to notice me squirming and in agony.

Uh, uh, uh. Not when the show is about to begin. Oh, don't worry I can't really hurt you, though it'll feel real. This is just like a pre-recorded television special... it happens as it happens, but oh, it'll all feel live enough.

God, I hadn't seen Auntie Sally since I was little. I forgot how much Dylan looks like her, that thick curly hair and the "don't fuck with me" accent she had, even though she was barely five feet. A spitfire with a voice like golden thread—nothing sounded as precious as Sally. I knew she retired from touring to perform small local gigs after having Dylan, but I never knew my mom had anything to do with that. Guess I was wrong.

As the singing began, it was hard to make out what song my mom and Sally were singing some blues-folk song. Though I could tell from the look on Marie, Oliver, and Anne's faces that it was a bittersweet melody. As my mom sang along, her eyes shined like sapphires, and I hate to say it, but they adored her up there.

This, sugar, this is what I wanted you to see. We loved your mother. We put faith in her, too. She was like this for a time, before Sally got into that car crash, then things started to change a bit. You must have been an itty-bitty thing then, probably never even saw this shine in her, huh? She could dazzle, that Laurie, she really could.

Growing up I knew mom spent all her time here, but I never thought much about whether or not she was happier working than raising me. I suspected she must have been but to see it—that's another story. As I look around, I see Marie hold Anne's hands and the two rest their heads atop one another, enjoying the song. Other residents clap and yell encore much too early but Sally and my mom just laugh and continue playing. I wish Dylan could see this, though he'd never believe it was real even if he was here in Matthew's memory.

You feel it, don't you? C'mon, c'mon tell me. Does it make you angry, Cara?

To know she had this capacity inside her, all along. Yet, she withheld that from me. Matthew clicks his tongue again, and again. I want to rip it out of his mouth, but I can't do anything but watch and listen.

My mom grabs the mic and looks directly at me, well, Matthew. "If you haven't had the chance to meet our new resident, Matthew, yet he's right over there. A little shy but he won't bite ladies!" The crowd chuckles, and I can feel something shift in the memory, a pulling back, whatever kindness she's showing him, Matthew doesn't want me to see it. He doesn't want to relive that, knowing how this story ends, what she does to him.

Well, let's not play this one out, Cara.

His hands clap twice.

Marie, Oliver, Anne, Sally, my mom, they all stay where they are. But I am being hurled backwards, further and further back until that vision is so small, I can't see it at all, not even a speck, not one hint of color. Again, I'm in the darkness. When I turn around, Matthew is ready to greet me with a twisted grin.

"Oh, I almost forgot," he says, then claps his hands twice.

The deepest exhale of my entire life leaves my body. It had felt so long since I spoke that I didn't know what to say first. Somehow the silence made it feel like whatever I said next had to have some sort of importance. I had all this time to think and be witty or clever or hurtful. But when this moment came, nothing comes out. In that memory, I felt a kind of begrudging recognition, how much it hurts to be irrevocably harmed by someone you love. "Look, I'm sorry for what my mom did," I say. "But Matthew, what does Beth have to do with it?"

"*This* is what you take away from my generous showing? You take all that history and then ask what it has to do with yours?" *Click, click, click* goes his tongue. "I truly thought that we'd have an inspired conversation, a meeting of the minds, an understanding of sorts to make all this a bit easier." He walks closer to me and lifts my chin upward. His eyes, now dark as charcoal, stare into mine and says "Oh, sugar, did you think this was going to be a negotiation? A grand reflection and then with some paltry words, I'd give Beth back?"

I weigh my next words carefully and settle on, "I guess I didn't think, did I?"

"Finally!" He claps, which makes all the nothing around us shake a bit, as if we stepped onto a fault line. "Some sense, I knew you had it in you, hehehe. Let's think, it's reason enough to think we want Beth because we want you, but why would we want you? C'mon, give it the ol' college try?" His fingers slide across my neck, grasping onto it, then lifting my entire body up, up, up. I struggle to breathe. "Why want you?"

I swing out my legs, trying to kick him. His grip tightens around my throat.

"Fuck you," I utter between gasps of breath.

"Oh, Cara, stop wasting my time with your sailor talk."

Matthew flings me feet away from him. My body drops onto the floor and sends this clattering sound through my skull, as if I fell onto a pit full of cymbals. The sound echoes and echoes, barraging my eardrums. Any harder, any longer, they'll burst. I can't take it. I can't it any of this anymore. "What do you want from me?" I scream, cradling my head in my hands. "Just tell me, what it is. What do you want from me? Just stop this."

"Why must you insist on ruining my fun? You give in so easily and all you think about is you or Beth and maybe Dylan, if Beth isn't around, but hadn't you paid attention to anything this whole time? Have you already forgotten about The Terror? Bless her heart, though I think it's a fool's errand living like how she does. Marie warned you about him. Remember? Not once did you even say his name. The gall of you, Cara. You don't even try to figure a thing or two out for yourself here. How have you even lived this long so far?"

When I pull my hands away from my head there is blood on my fingers. I touch my right ear and more trickles out. "I thought you said you couldn't really hurt me. What the fuck is happening to my ear?"

Matthew claps.

I scream, the sound, the pressure, it's building inside my ears, puffing out and out, making everything else around us sound like cotton balls as flashes of searing pain billow larger and larger. Then, a pop. A second of relief from the escape of the pressure gets replaced by a ringing sound, an impossible-to-escape sound echoing. Mucus and pus drain down the right side of my head. Everything grows a bit quiet, a bit muffled, garbled.

I want to pass out but Matthew claps again, awakening me with searing new pain.

After all, there are two ears.

"Please, please, I'll listen..." I sway back and forth and vomit. "Who is The Terror?"

Matthew smiles and claps three times. Suddenly the wooziness, the bile in my throat, the dull throbbing pain behind my ears, it all disappears. My hearing returns.

"He was my everything," he says. "There you go,

right as rain to meet him. 'Bout time too, as I need a long rest after our shenanigans. Enjoy the Play-Pen."

"That's where Beth is?"

"Yes," he says with a sinister curl of his lips. "Also, The Terror."

With that, Matthew claps his hands twice. Again, I fall into the darkness.

THE PLAY-PEN

Cara

"Sugar, open your eyes."

My back throbs. Somehow I fell onto a cement floor. Matthew looms above me, smiling so wide that his decayed root of gum sticks out. I can count how many teeth he's missing between the ones covered in tartar so thick I could pluck clumps of it out with tweezers. The thought churns my stomach, so it takes me a second or so to realize I'm not at my mom's house nor in Matthew's memories. We're somewhere new altogether.

Whatever it is, I have to face it if I have any hope of getting Beth back. I need to tell her. I'm sorry. Not like all the other times. Sometimes, I just fall so deep into all I can't do that that becomes all I am, just someone falling and falling, as if I can't do a thing to stop it, as if life just happens to me. This time, I'll stop it. I will.

"Where? What is all this?" I ask.

"I told you already. The Play-Pen. Really, you're a terrible listener, Cara." He shakes his head and pulls me to my feet. "Don't be shy. Have a look around, won't you? Don't you want to see where The Terror lives?"

The ceiling slopes downward, as if we're in a repurposed attic, so I can't quite see everything in the curved room at once. In front of me, there's a table with misshapen wooden chairs, the paint scraped off in areas like someone sharpened a knife along its edges. I stand to get a closer look. There is a set of antique plates and cracked teacups out with plates of towering fruit cakes and sugar cookies shaped like stars and hearts. In some of the chairs, there are stuffed animals with missing eyes. The centerpiece is made of melted dolls heads so that eyes poke out of ears and mouths, watching us, blinking. A dead mouse floats in the glass water pitcher.

Behind the table, there's a door painted a glittery yellow with globs of wet glue dripping off. The walls around us are white but have crayon scribbles drawn on them of smiling people missing heads or legs or fingers. On one area of the wall, there's a drawing of a small child sitting near a bedside crying and a nurse giving him a warm drink. But besides that, is a picture of a doctor with a bloody saw, cracking open a patient's chest.

What in the never, never land of fucking nightmares did I just walk into?

"Colorful, huh?" Matthew says, rubbing his hands together with delight.

"I don't see Beth anywhere. Take me to her."

"Oh, look who is too big for their britches, hmm?" Matthew points to the far corner of the room. "If you must know, she's there. Uh, uh uh," he says, grabbing my arm. "Not yet. Let's grab a snack. You must be famished after all that memory walking." When I turn around, he's dressed now in a white suit, looking like a carnival barker with a black cane. "Go on, it can't hurt to have a bite, huh? Then, we'll take you to her."

"You think I trust you? Let me go."

"No, but I know you're curious. You are a curious one, can't help but look even though you know you shouldn't. Bet that's why you stay around your mom so long, not knowing how she was woulda hurt more."

"Fuck you."

"Oh, the mouth on you needs some soap! But guess you'll have to settle for sugar." He puts both his hands on my shoulders, firmly pressing down. "Let's not spoil my fun. Have a cookie, won't you?"

"Where is —"

Matthew claps his hands and suddenly I'm in front of the table. He grabs a plate of sugar cookies and gestures for me to take one. I try to run but he claps his hands again and I'm sitting in a wobbly chair. He giggles at my surprise. "UGH, I'll take a dumb cookie. But tell me where Beth is. Have The Terror let her go."

"Sure, sure."

"Promise?"

"You have my word, darling. Benefits me just as much as you, in the end."

"Whatever you want me to do, I won't do it unless Beth is safe."

"Beth, Beth, Beth, I get it. You're in *love*, how charming, how absolutely banal. Oh, don't make that face. We both know she's going to leave you anyways. She always does. Yes, we've been chatting some. She has some *stories* about you. Now, be ever so kind and take a cookie. We worked so hard to make these for you."

I glance over the overflowing plates and grab a cookie shaped like a heart. That's what he wants, my pain and suffering. I know this will lead to some sick game but if that's what it takes to get Beth back, fine. I've felt worse than anything he can throw at me. If The Terror really is worse than him, I can't waste a single second. That could be lifetimes of torture for Beth. Besides, I've faced Matthew. I can face what or whoever he is and get her back. Who calls themselves The Terror anyway? They have to be overcompensating for something.

I bite into the cookie and swirls of vanilla and cinnamon hit my tongue. It's sweet, so sweet, so very sweet that I want more of it. I need more of it. I gobble one cookie down and then another. I have no idea the last time I ate but it feels like it's been days, months even. On my third one, a sharp pain hits my bottom jaw.

"Fuck! What is happening now…"

Matthew does nothing but smile.

"Are you trying to kill me? Is that what all this is?"

"Don't be silly, sugar, like I said, we *need* you. All this just gives me some amusement, see this here pain, the way you squirm and scream, it reminds me of what it feels like to *feel*, and I haven't felt in ages. Plus, as you might have figured, I have some bad blood with your mother. Well, all those wrathful feelings have to go somewhere! You don't mind now, darling? Promise I'll clap my hands and take it all away soon enough."

"Please, make it stop."

"I don't think I will yet. Still enjoying the taste of you, hehehe."

"I told you, I'm sorry. What my mom did, it wasn't her call to make." My jaw feels like it's being sawed in half. My gums throb as if a hundred pins were jammed into my mushy bits of mouth at once.

"Oh, you don't know the half of it. I trusted her, and she" he sighs. "No, no, Matthew, that is not your story to tell. It is his and I will not rob him of what he needs to say. He's been robbed of too much already."

The pain, it's like a needle twisting its way into my tooth. I hear a crack and feel the hole in the enamel widening, sending searing white-hot pain down my jawline. I spit out the sugary crumbs. When the crumbs fall onto the floor, they turn into squirming maggots. I stick my fingers in my mouth, swiping out any bit of sugary insect that's still in there. Oh fuck, that's gross. My teeth loosely rattle as I spit out flecks of bitten worms.

"Let me help with that," he says.

He sticks his dirty hand into my mouth and pulls out two of my back teeth with some of their red meaty roots still attached to the ends. Blood pools in my mouth, and I spit that out too onto the white floor.

"I know just where to put this!" He says, "See, my boy loves a good project. We've been redecorating lately if you can't tell." He waves his arms around, so deliriously proud. "This will be perfect for his door!"

Sweat pools down the back of my neck as I heave.

"Beth, Be-t-h. Where uh, fuck, oh fuck..."

Sure enough, Matthew takes my two teeth and sticks them to the glittery door. There's a *lot* of glue on that door. I wonder how many pieces of me will make it there and how many new ones I'll grow down here too. How long will Matthew drag this out? What if he never... no, no he needs me. He has to stop sometime. Soon. But the pain, oh god, the pain. I drop to my knees, resting my head on my thighs, staining my jeans with blood.

"We have a *theme* going on," he says. "But you and Beth are gonna do us a favor."

"Bring me, Beth," I spit out. "Now."

"Due time, I never go back on my word." He surveys the door. "Hmm, I think an ear would do rather nicely next, don't you? Well, I don't want to get ahead of myself. You know, as a parent, it's important you don't put your influence first. You must have an open mind and listen to what your child's heart of hearts wants."

"Ch-il-d?" I mumble through the spurts of blood, trying to stay focused and not pass out.

"Oh, you're mumbling is already annoying me to high heaven."

Matthew claps his hands. My mouth stops bleeding. I tongue the back of my jaw and feel the slick gloss of the newly formed pearly white teeth. Jesus, I wonder how many sets of teeth I'm going to lose today. For a moment, I wonder what Beth's time here might have been like, but I recoil at the thought. I can't. If I do, I'll just give up all hope on getting either of us, at least her, out of this mess alive. I slowly stand back up and face him.

"As I was saying, you'll be surprised by the lengths you go to for your child. Once they come into your life, it's like someone flipped a switch. Anything impossible can be made possible if it helps them succeed. Well, if they live long enough to, that is. Some of us aren't that lucky. No, you'd say we're rather cursed in that regard."

All of a sudden—the photo, Marie's story, Matthew's memory—it all connects. I know who The Terror is. But if I'm right, which I'm almost positive I am, that means my mother was a bigger monster than I thought. But she couldn't have, right? I mean I hate to say it, but I can kind of understand how the work broke her, growing attached to patients destined to die in weeks or a handful of years. You can't really help anyone so much as learn to teach them how to let go. To an extent, I get it. Maybe it might feel kinder to let someone go before it's so painful they have nothing left of themselves to hold onto at all. But this is something I never imagined she could do. Should I have? Growing up with her fits, I always wondered if she thought about it; killing. The look she'd get in her eyes, like a raging bull and the world was a matador. That's when I knew it was time to hide.

"Oh, did you finally get there, Jessica Fletcher? Took you long enough."

I exhale. "It's Lyle, isn't it?"

A kid. A little kid?

In a second, Matthew's head is in front of me. He grabs my neck and says, "Don't. Don't you ever say that name, especially not here. My son goes by The Terror now, that's a name he came up with himself. And here, in our world, he's the one pulling the strings. He gets what he wants. Of all of us, he's the youngest and most powerful and you will respect his name, sugar, or I will never let Beth go, even if she kicks and screams."

I raise my hands up. "Ok, ok, The Terror. He's here?"

Matthew lets me go and brushes off his shoulders. "Why yes, he's been preparing all day to meet you. Rather busy. Making sure he'd have a presentation of sorts for his delight, well in his meaning of the word."

"Is he with Beth?"

"Cara? Is that you?" A weakened voice calls out from the far corner of the room, an area draped in shadow. I can't see her, but I know the sound of that voice from anywhere. It's my Beth. She is here.

"Beth?!"

"Uh, uh, uh," he says. "Wait until The Terror calls for you. Beth can hang around longer."

"What do you mean by hang?"

"Oh, he's here. He just likes to watch. C'mon, Terror, let's not keep our guests waiting. That's rude behavior and we are proper here. Besides, it's about time you make your proposition known to Cara."

Slowly, the glittery door opens. Behind it, there's a boy no more than seven years old. He has an uneven bowl cut and is dressed in overalls with a blue and white striped shirt underneath. If he wasn't a tortuous ghost, I'd call him a cute kid. But the red stains on his sleeves sure are a huge minus. He tilts his head at me like a confused puppy, surveying me from side to side. When he speaks, his voice is soft as a whisper. I bend down to hear him.

"Wanna see a trick?" The Terror asks. How in the world am I going to face off with a kid? Matthew had to be fucking with me. There's no way that this child is worse than he was. How could he possibly be?

"I think I'll pass."

"Too bad, I'm gonna do it anyway."

The Terror flips his eyelids inside out, so the crimson veins show, a trick I used to do Dylan all the time to freak him out, pretending to be a zombie.

"Cute," I say. "But, uh, The Terror? I think we need to talk."

"Wait, wait, wait," he says, waving his hands up and down. "This is the best part!" He holds each eyelid in either hand. "One, two, three!" On three, his tiny hands rip the top eyelids off his face. He holds the flaps in his hands, shaking them. "Isn't this cool?" His irises are so brown that they almost melt into his pupils. The Terror flicks the half-moon-shaped skin onto the floor, and it sticks like spaghetti flung against the wall.

But he's not done. He sticks his fingers near the orb

of his eyes and pushes them into his skull. His fingers go deeper and deeper, up until his knuckle. His fingers hook around the optic nerve, ready to pull.

"Stop it!"

The boy falls to the floor with laughter, rolling back and forth. When he stands up again, his eyes look absolutely normal. "Oh, I got you. I got you! Oh, let's do it again. Oh, the look on your face. Let's go again."

"No, we need to talk, kid. I'm done with games." He runs over to me and holds my hands. I look to the floor and see his eyelids still there, shriveling up. The Terror whispers something to me but I can't hear him. I bend down and he gets a soft look. "Please don't go yet. Daddy is just mad, is all," he says. "I'm mad too. But I can't talk about it. It hurts too much. This is fun."

There's something about that look that I recognize; that brand of helplessness mixed with longing. I wonder if this is what Beth sees when she stares deeply into my eyes, how deeply unloved I feel all the time.

"L–, uh, I mean, The Terror, right?"

"Careful," Matthew says.

He nods excitedly as a bobblehead. "That's me! It's a big name for a big boy. What's next to play? Hmm, doctor? I have some tools. Beth is waiting for us over there." He points to the shadowy corner.

"Yes, yes, let's go see Beth."

"Ehem," Matthew says.

"But I want to play!"

They share a knowing look between them.

He sighs, "Fine. I just hate it there," he digs his heels into the floor.

"Good boy."

"What is it?"

"We have a plan," Terror says. "My memory walk time. Then, we play with Beth."

"No, no, no more of this. I need Beth first."

"Laurie is here, Cara."

My stomach drops. No, no, no.

"I can't see her."

"She needs to be punished for being bad and she's hiding. You're the only one she'll listen to," he says. As he speaks, the room gets darker and the temperature drops. I see my breath in the air. "You bring Laurie to me. Those are the rules. It's not fair that she dies and doesn't face us. It's not fair what happened to us."

Fuck.

"I don't, you don't understand. I *can't–*"

"You *will.*"

Lyle grabs both my hands and screams at the top of his lungs. "Enjoy the view," Matthew says, his voice drifting further and further away. I sink into Lyle's thoughts, and he lands us in a memory he'd rather forget.

A LOSS TOO BIG TO NAME

Cara

Holding Lyle's hands, I feel a sharper sense of dread. As we fall and fall into the darkness, his raspy screams sound like *believe me*. Something about him reminds me of a nightmare I had recently. When I found out my mom was dying, I had this reoccurring dream. I'd be in an apartment like mine, but not quite. Everything is where it's supposed to be, and yet, slightly off—a chair turned outward unlike how I left it, or a window cracked open despite knowing I closed it. I walk through rooms, noting the infinitesimal differences, then of course, doubt anything was wrong. Once I convince myself everything is fine, that I am fine, I sense someone standing in my bedroom, quietly studying me. When I peer into the room, no one is there. I turn around and feel someone rush behind me, close enough to breathe on the back of my neck. Each step I take, it follows. It pauses when I do like my shadow came to life but couldn't sever the cord between us. A marionette. Eventually, I turn around in the nick of time to catch it before it darts away. I see someone wearing my face, smiling at me.

Those twisted lips. That look of knowing something—better, smarter, a fucked-up kind of fortune teller. I yell and yell, but she just stands there, observing me berate and push someone, but not me. When I give up fighting, which I always do, she waves. I fade away into nothingness, and the last thing I see is her hand waving goodbye. By the time my vision sees nothing but blackness, I wonder if I was the shadow all along.

The look in Lyle's eyes reminds me of that kind of pain that shakes all you know about what's real. He looks almost giddy to show me his memory but in a sad and desperate way, like a fish out of water flopping so hard, praying those actions will return it to the relief of home. In his eyes, I see that hope. I can tell he can't hold this memory alone anymore. He needs me to see it to understand. I know I should be scared. If I'm to trust anything that Matthew told me, I should be terrified. But I think I'm like him. His hands are so small. They feel too small to have had to carry that much pain. His fingers grip mine tighter, and he whispers, "We're here."

I look to his hands and see dried blood under his fingernails; a reminder to stay cautious.

As the colors and objects in the room come into focus, I realize we're in my mom's kitchen. Decades earlier. The tile floors aren't cracked, and the cupboards aren't falling off their hinges. No dirty dish in a mile radius. I let go of Lyle's hands and take it all in, running my hands against the countertops, impressed at how they glide and aren't interrupted by grime. There's even a lemon scent from a candle filling the room. The last time I saw the house this tidy was right around the time I left for college. Around then, we weren't speaking—me and mom. There was a fight about me leaving the state and it got ugly, making me determined to cut ties.

At least, for a couple of years or so. That's how it went until my hope buoyed up again.

"Lyle? What is all this?"

"Where I died," he said. "Don't call me that or you'll never see Beth."

"Ok, ok... But here? You died here?"

He hung his head. "Laurie took care of us when Dad got too sick."

That takes me by surprise. I didn't know that my

mom brought a patient home, never mind one with his son. Was she that lonely when I left? Did she really need to replace me with *more* patient time? At the very least, she could have said something, anything about it. If I had known, maybe I could have helped them. And why my mother? Didn't they have any other relatives who could have helped? Or pooled together money to have him in a memory care facility? How is she supposed to give around-the-clock care when she works full-time?

But all I can say is "I, I didn't know."

Lyle shrugs. "Already dead. Laurie said Dad had not enough money left, so we stayed here for no money. No one visited us. We weren't here long. A winter. Had a lot of chicken noodle soup and crackers."

"Where did you stay?"

Lyle grabs onto my wrist and pulls me down the hallway. We stop short at the guest room. The door is shut, but I can hear voices inside. I hear my mother talking softly to someone. He tugs on my sleeves. "There," he says. "But I don't want to go in. You go. I know what happens. I don't like to come here. It hurts too much."

"Ok."

I take a deep breath and open the door. On the other side, I see my mother tending to Matthew. He's not like the Matthew I saw. He's shrunken down, half the size at least—all bone and skin. He keeps trying to roll into the fetal position, but it hurts him. With each movement, he moans. There must be a bedsore, something that happens when the body doesn't move enough. Blood collects, tissue dies, and you're left with living rot. Mom had one too, despite the stretching of her legs. She favored one side too much. We couldn't stop it.

I look at Matthew curling into himself like a child. The older you get, the more your body regresses. It's really fucked up. Time only allows a degree of growth and once you pass it, everything breaks down, getting smaller, weaker. Your blood travels slower. Synapses stop firing in the brain. There are longer and longer moments between breaths. Your lungs will decide for you when enough is enough. Did you know you can count the moments between breaths to estimate how much longer someone has left in this world? I did it for mom, holding her hand. The chest rose and dropped. Rose and dropped. Rose and then it never did drop, did it?

My mom gives up combing Matthew's hair and tells him to relax. He doesn't listen, but by the look of him, I don't think he can understand much of anything. Like what Matthew told me, he's trapped inside his body and pleading for a way out. Old age is rarely kind. Lyle sits at the foot of the bed watching them. He's quiet and rocking back and forth. Besides them is a small table filled with things—briefs, sanitizer wipes, gloves, aloe gel, clean sheets, pads for the bed, and a package of unopened syringes. Lyle goes to the table and starts fiddling with things.

"Will this help?" He asks, holding a package of bandages. My mother sighs and shakes her head.

"No wounds are open," she says, as if a child can understand that.

"Oh," he says, lowering his head, disheartened.

"We just have to make him comfortable," she says.

With that, Lyle kisses Matthew on his forehead. "There," he says.

My mom smirks, pulling her tight curls up into a sloppy bun. There's sweat on her forehead, likely from needing to lift and move his body up and over so much of the time. I know that look too. One time I had to give CPR for a half an hour and couldn't move my arms right for a week. This work is bodily work; it's in the bones kind of work. You give and you give so much of yourself to help someone be. She looks so incredibly tired. The bags of her eyes have bags, and she can't stand still for more than a moment, fussing over this and that.

As he snores, I see his missing teeth and wonder at

what point someone stopped noticing that he had others? At what point, did someone like my mom decide that it was good enough? That he didn't deserve to have floss or mouthwash. The thought fills me with so much anger, my hands start shaking. It's one thing to see him like this as a ghost but an entirely different thing to remember that this is how he looked up until his death. Maybe a part of me deserved to have my teeth ripped out by their roots, for looking at him how I did.

Why didn't anyone else notice? Why didn't anyone else visit her? Him? Them?

She takes Matthew's wrist to measure his pulse. Lyle interrupts her. "Will he wake up soon? He's been sleeping all day." My mom hushes him, and Lyle goes back to fingering the boxes of supplies, reading them as if the right box will help his dad's decline. It won't. I can tell from my mother's look that she knows there is not long left. Days, maybe. Likely, less than a week. His hands are too blue-tinted, which means not enough oxygen is getting to his limbs. She takes his pulse again and shakes her head. "What if I sing him a song?" Lyle asks.

"Lyle, please," she says.

"But I want to talk to him. We haven't talked all day, it's not fair."

"He needs rest, ok?"

"But he's rested enough," he says, throwing a box on the floor. "I want to talk to him."

Lyle goes over to Matthew and gently shakes his shoulders, which only makes his moaning worse. "Stop," my mom says. "Lyle, stop it. You're going to upset him and at this stage, comfort is what he needs most. Stop." My mom pushes Lyle away from him, sending him onto the floor. His eyes swell up with tears, readied to explode. "Now, now, I didn't mean that, and you know that. Lyle, control yourself. You need to for your father."

I want to scream. He is seven years old, mom. Seven. But she can't hear me.

"You never let me sing to him," he huffs, and crosses his arms. "Never, ever, ever."

There it is. The look in her eyes, that last straw. I've seen it thousands of times. I know what comes next will be heartless and targeted to do the maximum amount of damage. Lyle, no one is ready for that.

"Because he won't hear you, Lyle? He can't tell you're here."

Lyle gives up holding his tears back. He wails and wails as his father moans and moans—a symphony of loss. Whatever patience is left in my mom disintegrates. She throws up her hands and screams, "You don't get it. I'm trying. No one else is doing anything but I am trying here. I am trying so hard. No one gets it. I'm so alone."

"He's my dad," he wails. "It's not fair."

"I just need some quiet."

The moaning, the crying, it continues. The sound is getting to her, I can see it.

Laurie takes her hair down and runs her fingers through each strand, tugging it, clenching fistfuls of hair in her grasp. Her eyes go to the table. She picks up the opened box of syringes and takes out three of them. She bends down beside Lyle. "Ok, ok," she says. "It's time for daddy's medicine. How about I go make you some cocoa too? Will that make it better? Something sweet to help the medicine go down. Like Marry Poppins?"

"Marshmallows, too?" Lyle asks, rubbing his swollen red eyes with the back of his sleeves.

"Yes, yes, of course," she says. "Then you both can take a nice long nap. Who knows? Maybe you'll wake up together and then you can sing him your song, ok? Wouldn't that be nice to wake up to?"

Lyle nods.

The door to the guest room slams shut.

Lyle's ghost returns. In his hands, he holds a cracked teacup.

"This is what she gave me. After that, I went to sleep.

I didn't wake up. I was too loud. She just wanted quiet but now I can't stop screaming. That's why Dad built me the Play-Pen. I can scream and scream and no one ever tells me to calm down."

"Didn't anyone come looking for you?"

At that, Lyle's eyes sharpen. "Did you?"

"No, I mean, like the police? Child services? Anyone?"

Lyle shrugs again and crushes the tea-up in his hands. Porcelain shards stick out of his hand, but he squeezes his fist tighter, spilling blood onto swirls of water-color painted roses and gold trimmings. "Who would ask about me, the foster kid with a dead dad? Laurie didn't tell anyone I was here, so I never was."

"She couldn't have gotten away with that. There's no way in hell —"

Lyle laughs and slaps his knees. "That's funny."

"What is?"

Lyle drops the cup onto the floor and holds my hands in his. "You're just like Laurie. You never listen. You talk, talk, talk, talk. I'm tired of talk. Bring Laurie to me or I won't let Beth go. Nope, nope, nope."

"I can't. You don't understand, I can't face my mom."

"Bye-bye, Beth then!"

"Lyle, this isn't a game. Laurie is dead but Beth is still alive. You can help her."

Lyle snaps his fingers. My spine cracks and I fall to the floor. I can't feel my legs or arms or raise my head. I can blink but that's about it. My mouth moves but no scream comes out. I try to kick but nothing works.

"Silly, everything is a game. Didn't daddy tell you? I don't think you heard him. My game, my rules. Why don't we go play with Beth, so you won't ever ever forget who is in charge. Not you or your mom."

Lyle screams, sending us back to the Play-Pen.

THE ONE WHO LISTENS

Cara

When we return, I'm able to move again. But the first thing I see causes me to stagger backward. My Beth is nailed to pieces of plywood with her arms and legs outstretched. Next to her, there's a blackboard. Someone drew a hangman figure but it's missing its hands. On the board, there are three white dashes between two letters *s* and *e*. Lyle smiles besides it, with a piece of white chalk in his hand. "Can you guess what word?"

"I'm tired of guessing wrong," Beth moans. "So tired." Her left and right hand are on the floor. Blood drips onto the cement from her stumps like the pitter patter of rain. "A?" All the air goes out of my lungs. My Beth. Terror jumps up and down excitedly, then fills in the missing letter so the mystery word reads: s _ a _ e.

Matthew pats Terror on his shoulder. "My good boy," he says. "Let's show Cara our game, shall we?" Near the board is a tray filled with tools, pliers, a buzzsaw, a hammer, a bloody knife, and a half-used box of nails. Beth's eyes flutter open. She finds me. "Cara, please, please. You can stop this. Stop all of this."

"Beth!" I run to her, but Matthew claps his hands. Suddenly, my legs are stuck. I can't reach her though everything in me is pushing my body toward her. *Fuck*, he wants me to watch this. He wants me to feel how powerless I am here. To bathe in the knowing that I roped Beth into my mess *again*. My hands reach out to her but grasp nothing but air. "Beth, I'm so, so sorry. I didn't mean, god…I'll figure it out, I will! I'll save you." Beth looks at me with eyes so cold that I know once we leave here, I'll never see her again. I know I deserve that. But she must understand why I can't face her, why it's not so easy, why I'd rather stall and bargain. Some people can destroy you with one word. Just the sound of their voice decimates your insides into bits. When I see her, I become a child. I seek permission to find punishment. I can't help myself. She was supposed to be gone. It was supposed to be over. But now? I don't think I'll ever be rid of her and that's a much more terrifying thought than anything else these ghosts have shown me. I'd rather rip each fingernail off my finger.

"What else can I give you?" I ask. "Me? My life? Take it. Not worth much anyways."

"See," Matthew says. "We have all the time in the world here. We don't need to kill you, but we can make you wish you were dead, Cara. That you felt the god-awful nothingness that we did." He strolls around Beth as she squirms on the wooden planks. He drags a finger down her arm, tracing her milky flesh. "Then we'll snap our fingers and you, Beth, will be good as new. But you'll still remember what it felt like to be on the brink."

"Guess again!" Terror squeals.

I stare at the letters, and it hits me. "The word is shame," I say.

"Hey!" Terror says. "No fair. It's Beth's turn. We'll just have to start all over."

"No!" Beth screams.

Matthew claps. Beth's hands are still on the floor, palms facing upward, as if wanting someone to hold them. But Beth's body now has a new set of hands on it. At the sight of them, Beth starts to weep. "Not again."

"That's my favorite part," Terror says. He walks over to Matthew and hugs his knees. Matthew pats him on the back and smiles. "And then, we do it all again! We do it again and again and again and again!"

"Truly is delectable. People always say worse things can happen, sugar, but what do you do after the worse has already happened to you, hmm? We, Terror, and me, we want you to live with that. Death is too easy."

"Beth hasn't hurt you," I say. "You know this is cruel, right? Laurie hurt you. Not her."

"Leverage is a gorgeous thing. You can't face your mother, boo-hoo, we'll just have to watch you face this over and over until you can." He twirls his black cane in the air. "Consequences are to be deeply felt."

"Then let me feel them," I say. "Pluck out my eyes! Take all my teeth! I don't care."

"Too late. You should have visited your mother sooner. You should have seen that she had too much on her plate. You could have called child services. You could have saved my boy. Instead of wasting your life in bars."

"Please, just..." Beth starts to say but something changes. Her head goes slack. For a second, I think that she passed out. But when her head rises, her eyes are glistening white orbs. "We've had enough silly games, my boys," Marie says. "What a pity you let this get so far, it's like you've just been dead yesterday. Let her go."

"Marie?" I ask. "How did you...?"

The white orbs stare at me. "Once an invite's given, the door stays open. I don't like to be rude, but I figure she'd rather me deal with this now. Boys, as I've said so kindly, it's time to stop these shenanigans."

"That's not fair, Marie!" Terror says. "We *need* Laurie, and this will help."

"Child, has any of your games worked so far? I don't see Laurie anywhere in this, now do you?"

Matthew's upper lift curls into a snarl. "Well, things take time, persistence, and dogged determination! Where have you been all this time? Certainly not putting in the hard work that we have been doing, hehehe."

"Oh, please, Matthew. You know as good as me that

you're taking out all that anger, all that pain on the wrong person here. Yes, we have lots to say to Laurie, but this isn't how you get that chance. *You're* stalling too."

"Ha! Well, what do you propose I do differently then, huh?"

"Simple. All of this has always been rather simple. Just ask the girl why she doesn't want to see her mother and listen. Why do you think I visited her in the first place? I believe in her. She can help us."

She's not wrong, though I'd never say that aloud. What a silly thing to say: I'm scared of my mom. Try it out. People will imagine earthquakes and erupting volcanoes and crashing planes. They'll point to those uncontrollable situations with disastrous results and say *that*, now *that*, is something worthy of your fear. A mother? What harm can a mother do? What they don't understand is it's not the harm. Not at all. Yes, there's that. Bu that's not what haunts me. The fear is what *she* has done to the core of me. The fear is that I'm emptied out. I'll spend my entire wasted life searching for what can fill the black hole of my soul. Along the way, I'll run everyone who tries to love me into the ground because that's all I know how to do. For some, a mother is a wound that never fully heals. I never asked for that. But did it matter? Will I ever matter? I'll look at cookie cutters and think of old scars not warm-fuzzy yuletide greetings. Thrown plates. Stained dishtowels. Place a hand on my shoulder and watch how high, how quickly I jump into the air. The root of me is rotted.

"I'm not scared!" Terror says, stomping his little feet. "I'm mad."

"Ah, yes, anger. Anger is a funny thing, isn't it? A way to turn all that sadness and fear outward, so you don't have to feel it in you, seething, dragging you down with it. Anger is a fool's errand, my dear, dear Lyle."

Terror shakes his little fists. "Marie, you know I don't go by that anymore."

"Why? Because it hurts you to remember? You don't know what to do with that, do you? None of you do. We've been watching all this and keeping quiet because we thought, well, maybe you'd all see it in time."

"See what?" I ask.

Marie sighs. "We thought you'd see that you're not on opposing sides here. Can't you feel how Cara has been hurt? I know you can. I know you feed on that. But what if, hear me out boys, you stopped punishing her for Laurie's mistakes? You want to see Laurie, want a big ol' showdown, you trust Cara to get you there. You let Beth go, and you do whatever it takes to support Cara, so she opens that door. She's the only one that can."

"Door? What door?" I ask.

Matthew sighs. "Marie, this is all too sentimental. Why don't we —"

"Matthew, you've had your fun. Gotten out that rage. But I know deep-down what you want more than anything is to have your boy rest. Not do all this," she waves her hands. "You want to rest with him, too."

"Maybe... I'll give you that, maybe, we got our calculations a lil' wrong, skewed. Perhaps we laid it on a bit thick, but fear motivates. Fear of losing who we love *is* a grand motivator, Marie. Can't you understand?"

"So does wanting answers," she says. The words make Matthew's tirade pause.

"Dad?" Terror asks. "What are you doing?"

"We're tired, my boys, let us all rest," Marie says.

Beth's head goes slack again. She starts to moan softly.

When I look at Matthew, his black cane and carnival barker attire are gone. He's just a man with a faded baseball cap and worn-in jeans. He paces back and forth, sitting on Marie's words. After some time, he nods quietly to himself and claps his hands. With that, Beth is no longer hanging. She cries out, this time with something close to relief. She walks over to me with tears streaming down her face, waiting for me to speak.

"Beth, I'm sorry."

"Are you? Do you have any idea what this was like for me?"

"No, no, I don't. I couldn't." I exhale. "Matthew, can she go home?"

"Wait, Cara, what are you going to do?" Beth asks, grabbing my arm. I shake it off.

"Something I should have done from the start. But not here, not with you. This has never been about you, any of it. I think it's time for you to let this, let us go. We're not good for each other. We know that. Don't look at me like that. This isn't like before, I'm not saying this *only* so you feel compelled to stay. I mean it, we can't do this. I can't continually hurt you because I haven't yet dealt with my own shit. I can't do it again."

Beth nods and bites her bottom lip. "Ok."

"Ok."

"Beth," Matthew says. "It's been a pleasure, sugar, but it's time for you to go."

"Dad!"

"Lyle," he says. "Marie is right. You can't understand it and you don't have to but remember how you told me you just can't stop screaming? Can't stop tearing the heads off of dolls? I can make it stop, all of it, and we can get that nap you always wanted, and you can sing me all the songs in all the world. Would you like that?"

Lyle asks, "But what if we don't wake up together?"

Matthew kneels by Lyle and holds his hands. "Oh, Lyle, we're too determined not to, so we will. Eventually, but before then, we'll get to rest. After we talk with Laurie, we'll get to finally have some sleep. We haven't slept in over twenty years! Aren't you, now don't lie to me, just the *littlest* bit tired, son? C'mon?"

Lyle sways back and forth and mumbles, "Yeah, yeah, I am."

"Then that settles it. Ready, Beth?"

Beth nods.

"Wait! Will she be ok?" I ask.

"Yes," he says. "She'll wake up in her car and this will all feel like a terrible nightmare. To her, it might as well be. But I don't think she'll mind that, after what we put her through, wouldn't you say so, Beth?"

"I want to forget all of this more than anything. I need this to be over."

"See? She'll be just fine, but I wouldn't expect her to call you anytime soon to chat. Who wants to go on a date with nightmare fuel?" With that, Matthew clapped his hands. Beth, my Beth, vanishes from sight. After she left us, the room shifts. The crayon colors on the wall melt down until the room's walls are black. The chairs vanish next, and then the melted dolls' heads, and the treats, as if the world was being sucked into a vacuum. Poof after poof! In minutes, all the knives and nails and splattering of blood disappear from our view.

I'm left with Lyle and Matthew in a dark, dark room. Not just black but the kind of darkness where you can't make out shapes or colors. You can't tell the curve of the wall. There is no wall. There are no curves or lines. There's just a mass of unmovable nothingness. Here, we stood quietly for a bit, getting our bearings, letting Marie's words sink into all our skins. I'm not sure how long we stand there but after what feels like decades, a white door appears in the distance. "What's that?" I ask. Matthew and Lyle look at each other.

"That, sugar, is where she is. We can't go in until you do. We've tried, trust me, we've tried. But it won't open. We did this, all this, to get you here to open it for us. After you do, we can finally be at peace."

"Cara?" Lyle's voice squeaks. "Will you please help us?"

His little eyes plead with feelings too big to name. I can tell he's sorry and confused but doesn't know how to tell me either. Instead, he just starts to quietly cry. It reminds me of when I cried as a child. My mom hated the sight. She'd send me into my room, so she didn't have to hear the sound, what want or need I had.

I bend down and wipe the tears from Lyle's cheeks. "It's ok," I say. "Sometimes, when we have these big, big feelings, we do things. Strange things. We hurt ourselves. Hurt others. We don't mean to do it, do we?"

Lyle shakes his head and wipes his eyes on his sleeves. "No," he says.

"She's behind that door, you're sure?"

"Sure as we can be," Matthew says. "But we've heard her voice, so we think, yes. Yes, she's there. If you go in, we'll let you go home. Go back to whatever it is you were doing. But you see now, if you don't, Lyle will be in pain forever, for all of eternity. If my hunch about you is right, then you know how there's nothing worse in the world than a suffering child that no one can hear or see and wants so badly just to be told it's all ok?"

I exhale. Fuck.

I stare at the door in front of me. I think through all that's happened and all that could. I replay and replay the past few days in my head. My fingers grasp the cold doorknob, lingering there. I can't remember the last time I slept without a nightmare. Maybe this will be something that'll give me the chance to dream again. No terrors. No jumping at the sound of the wind blowing. No nervous stomach that can't handle anything spicy or salty or sweet or really anything delicious at all without giving me heartburn. Maybe this *is* it, my way out. My way through. My way to letting go of that Cara, that fraction of a human walking around up there.

"Ok," I say.

Lyle tugs on Matthew's sleeve. Matthew bends down to hear Lyle's whispers. "Ah, ok, ok." He stands back up and faces me. "As an apology, we'll let you go on in first. Say what you need to say, and we'll follow after. Lyle says it's the least we can do so that you don't have to hurt as much anymore. That fine by you, Cara?"

I nod.

"Settles it, then, what are you waiting for?"
I turn the doorknob and push the door open.

***

Here. I am finally here.

"Hello?"

WHAT'S LEFT TO SAY

Cara

There's a white flash. Suddenly, I'm outside my mother's house—decades earlier. I can tell because the pool covering hasn't been torn up yet by squirrels. The plant beds are still in their neat little rows. Our fence hasn't rotted yet. As the sun hits the back of my neck, I search for her. Besides our oak tree and a rocking swing, there's a plot of magenta mums. There she is. Those were her favorite flowers to plant. Always a sucker for perennials. She liked them because, unlike annuals, these kinds of flowers always grew back. She liked to say that meant something as if they kept notice of her hard work. Their growth was a promise that did something right.

On her knees, she shoves the trowel into the dirt. Every couple digs or so, she wipes the sweat off her forehead with the back of her hand. I don't think she even notices I'm here. But it's like she could read my mind. The second I think that she turns her head to face me. My chest tightens. Thoughts flood my brain about what to say next. Before she died, I hadn't talked to her in years. In the few weeks I visited her on hospice, she couldn't really tell the difference between me and the other nurses that'd visit to check her vitals. She was in and out of consciousness. They said it got into her brain. If I had come months earlier, it would have been different. But to her, then, I was no one. They said she never went to a doctor's until she couldn't stand without coughing blood.

I remember the look they gave me and the glances between them. I imagine their conversations about me when I wasn't in the same room. Where was her daughter? Why didn't she live with her? I imagined the questions they'd want to ask, and the demands hinged on them. It couldn't have been that bad between you. Does she know she only gets one mother? Life is short, and she'll never know she was here. She never got a goodbye.

"Oh," my mom says. "It's you." She stands and brushes the dirt off her knees. Her neck flushes red with a sunburn. Her brown sunhat shields half of her face in shadow and her black curls stick all over the place with frizzy sweat. "Well, don't just stand there? Are you gonna help me or not?"

But that wasn't the right question to ask. She, I, we always knew the answer to that. I thought a lot about what I always wanted to ask or tell her if I had the chance. It all came down to one impossible question.

"Why?"

I don't know if any answer I receive will be good enough, but I have to try. For me, for Lyle, and for the endless wondering about what I did or didn't do. I need to know, deep down, it's not my fault. That I did all I could to make us work. That me leaving her to spend her last days alone was the right thing to do for everyone. If I stayed, we'd only fight, and it'd get bad again. I'd stab holes in her wine boxes so she wouldn't drink, and she'd punch a hole through the door. Locks would lose meaning. She'd swallow my voice whole, so I'd live in the belly of her. I'd be as good as a doll. A plaything. A shoebox to carry all her regrets. And why would I stay? For the littlest moments, when she'd smile at me, I believed that she loved me in her own way. I'd starve myself for a scrap of love, and that's no way to live. That's no way to be a daughter. That's a sentence to become a ghost.

Her brows furrow in confusion. "Why what, Cara? These mums won't rotate themselves."

I've had my teeth pulled from my jaw. I've had my ears smooshed to mucusy bits. A child cut off the hands of my ex-girlfriend. A bed, a fucking bed, sent my best friend in the world into a coma. In my dreams, at least I fucking hope it was my dreams, a ball of black smoke blew up my body from the inside out, but this?!

This is what sends me over the edge. The nerve.

I scream so loud my entire body shakes. I kick over one of her dumb statues of a clown. Who puts a stone clown statue in a garden anyway?

"Are you fucking kidding me? WHY?! Why, what? Why, everything?"

"If you're going to be like that, go to your room," she says, turning from me and attending to her plants again. Dismissed. There she wants me to drift off, as threatening to her as a fucking paper plane hitting her. Even in death, I'm a swatted housefly. If I have no use to her, then I am of no use, I am to be stored away.

"No."

"Don't speak that way to your mother," she says, shooting me a glance as cold as steel.

"No, no, no, no," I say, rushing over to her. My heart beats so fast in my chest that it might burst, might pump so hard that the rest of me can't take the pressure and explodes into a splattering of flesh all over her precious mums. "We are going to talk. You don't get to ignore me now. You're dead. You understand that?"

"Of course, I'm not an idiot."

"Well, then, talk. We talk. What else have you got to do?"

She sighs and throws her shovel onto the amber stone walkway. "Well, spit it out then, what is it?"

"I…"

"I'm listening."

"First —"

"Oh dear god, there's a list?" She picks up her shovel and starts to dig around the plant's roots, shifting a flower this way and that. Every once in a while, the metal hits a rock and makes a chattering sound.

"You said you'd listen."

"Might as well work as I do," she says. "No use wasting time."

Should have known that even her ghost would value herself above all else.

"Fine, tell me why you killed Lyle. The others, I can kind of understand, but him?"

This makes the digging stop. She pauses, then pulls the hat over her eyes more. "Don't act like I'm some mastermind. That's not how it happened, and you shouldn't talk about things you don't understand."

I bend down and pull the trowel from her hands. "Then make me understand."

She turns away from me and picks up the watering can, dripping beads of moisture onto the petals and dirt. "I didn't plan it. I was tired. Do you know how hard it is to work full-time and go home to all that?" The water keeps coming and the soil soaks up each drop. "I didn't mean to do that. I meant to give him a little morphine like what you give a bad toothache. He was inconsolable. I just needed him to sleep for a little.

"To sleep? So you drugged him?"

"Oh, when you say it like that, it sounds awful. Everything is a drug. Coffee is a drug. Chocolate and cheese is a drug that gives you a feeling like being on cocaine. At least that's what the brain does. It wasn't like that. The measurements were off, is all." She keeps pouring water onto the flowers, even though it's starting to overfill the bed, turning the dirt into sloshy manure.

"Could have happened to anyone, Cara. Anyone."

"It didn't happen to anyone. You caused it. Can't you hear yourself?"

She clicks her tongue and picks up the garden rake. The metal prongs scratch and scratch the soil until their roots tangle in its grasp like a hand clawing and clawing until the plants rip apart from one another. "I was just tired, so very, very tired. I didn't have any help. I had to do it all by myself—the changing, the toenail cutting though he'd punch me in the face sometimes. The feeding... It was like having two babies at home. I tried calling you at home, but you were in one of those moods of yours. You never did call me back, you know. Hmmm."

Unbelievable.

"Why did you even do it? And how the hell didn't anyone catch you?"

"Stop it," she spat. "Don't make me sound like a murderer."

"You are."

With that, she spins around and shoves me to the ground. "I'm a caretaker," she says. "You think it's easy, huh? Being the one who had to raise you alone? Had to care for hundreds of patients each day with seldom a break? To get endless calls from their families when someone was sick. Oh, did Denise eat today? We'd love to take her out to lunch as a surprise. Well, fucking Denise can't swallow more than applesauce so best of luck with that," she continues and picks up her rake. She goes back to clawing the dirt apart, shredding the leaves and mushing the petals together into the soaked ground. "It never ended. And who took care of me? No one. What did I get? My sister died in a car crash on her way to go sing to my patients. I have a nephew who couldn't even go to my wake. He blames me, you know. Oh, but I bet you two talk about me all the time. Blame me for everything. It's your mother's fault. How simple. How Freudian. Doesn't that make it so much easier for you to ruin your life if I'm always the bad guy? That's what you want, isn't it? Still, you're such a child."

My eyes sting with tears. I stand back up. I will not let her take control of this conversation as she's done with so many others. This will not be how we last talk to each other. I will not be reduced to someone invisible.

"You never answered my question," I say. "How did

you get away with it?"

She turns from me and takes her rake to the oak tree. In the middle of the trunk, I carved my initials as a kid. She takes the rake and starts slashing away at C. G. Metal grinds into the wood, sending woodchips this way and that. "What a mess you leave everywhere you go. Even here. Cara gets to do whatever she wants."

"Answer me."

The rake curls up the wood, splintering it. Deeper and deeper the rake digs into the tree. Then the rake soaks into her hands, disappearing from sight. No matter. She uses her fingernails to scratch and scratch the wood. "You're a nurse, you should know better. Don't think they do autopsies on the elderly. You know that. At that stage, it's all about comfort. Elderly patients even die of undiagnosed cancer because they're afraid of the risks that operating would do to someone so fragile. Matthew was gonna die anyway and he was in pain."

The middle fingernail on her right-hand breaks off. "Lyle? Incidental. Foster kids often are. Matthew should have known better than to start fostering someone at sixty years old. But he was naive and lonely and selfish. I did him a favor. Lyle had awful parents. I gave him a way out, a kinder way to die, than the system."

Tears fall down my cheeks as I watch fingernail by fingernail pop off her hand like the cap on a beer can. Blood pours between her fingers, down her wrists, and into the ground. But she won't stop clawing the tree.

"Stop, mom, stop."

"No, you said you wanted to know. If you're gonna be an adult, you'll have to listen."

Scratch. Scratch. Scratch. Flesh on the top of her fingers peel against the pressure but she doesn't stop. She doesn't listen. It takes everything in me not to fling myself on her and hold her. I don't want her like this.

But it's not my choice to make for her anymore, to clean up. I'm here to learn the truth.

"Ok," I say. "Tell me."

"I told the police he went missing. Do you think they spared much time looking for a foster kid, hmm? He'd already run away from five previous families. Oh, they thought I was a saint taking both of them in when I did. You weren't there. You don't know. But the cops? They gave me a Dunkin Donuts gift card for my trouble."

I hear a bone crack, then two, but she won't stop scratching. Crack, crack, crack. I remind myself that these are her hands, not mine. I look down at my hands and double check all my fingers are still there.

They are. I breathe a sigh of relief.

"I won't hurt you, Cara," she says. "I've never hurt you, but you always act like I did. You don't know how good you had it." Her pointer finger bends back so far from the scratching it can touch her wrist. The scratching continues and the bark looks more red than beige now. There goes a thumb, flopping to the side.

"That's not true."

"Believe what you want."

"Why," I choke back tears, refusing to have her see me weep. "Why do you do this to me? Why don't you just see it? Can't you just finally admit that you're the child, here? That I've always looked after you?"

"I did my best," she says.

Still, she scratches, peeling back more wood and flesh. Crack, crack, crack.

"It wasn't good enough."

Then the scratching stops. She turns to face me and holds my chin with her mangled fingers. "I know. But the thing about being a mother is you can't take it back once it happens. You just have to live through it."

There.

I look into her eyes and see a version of what I always saw, when she looked at me, was a life, lifetimes, even a multiverse of everyone else she could have been if I had never been born. That weight, that pressure, that colossal why is all I ever wanted her to admit. But even now, I knew in my bones, she'd never have the courage to admit it.

"I tried," she said. "You won't understand until you have a child of your own."

"I don't want to understand that." I wipe the tears from my eyes.

"Oh," she says, dropping my face with a sigh. "All women eventually do." She kneels down back to her mums. "I want to get back to my garden. Give me this? Not much else I have left. This is all I have left of me."

"That's it?"

She picks up her trowel and starts whacking the dirt again. She can't even look me in the eyes when she says what hurts the most. "Cara, you, and I both know whatever I say will not give you what you really want. What you can't seem to admit is that you don't want me, you don't even like me. You want who I never was."

My initials on the oak tree are gone. What's left of the curve of the C has a fingernail stuck into it; like she cut me right on out of the belly of that trunk. Maybe, in a way, I have been cut out—severed from her. I have been. This whole time. I have been. But still looking to hold onto something, some chance, some potential.

But there's not one here.

I steady my nerves and say, "Goodbye, momma."

"You never answered my call," she mumbles. "Cara never answers my calls."

She doesn't look up from what she's doing. Whack, whack, whack goes her shovel. Whatever she's digging for, I know she will never find it. I know she will never have what wishes of joy or purpose she had as a kid with records on her bed. She liked The Carpenters just like her sister. Oh, they dreamed of being like them too, going on the road, singing melodies to stadiums of fans with names in lights. But her sister isn't here. No one is. She's alone. She's pushed everyone else away from her, even in death, she is alone. As much as she wants to be right, she'll keep digging and scratching at everything else before she forgives herself for who she became.

I can't forgive her. But I can forgive myself for imagining I could. Maybe one day she'll face herself. But that's not my job to keep tabs on anymore. It's my job to release myself from these ghosts. "Lyle, Matthew, Marie, Anne, Oliver," I call out. "I found her." Whatever happens next, it's their job to sort through, not mine. Within seconds, I see the shapes of her patients return. Even Oliver becomes corporeal with his mismatched socks and steady gait. Each one nods at me, and I nod back. Everyone deserves a chance to find answers.

I hope that whatever they need from her they'll receive it too.

My mother won't turn around to face them. She keeps shoveling as they surround her. But they're growing impatient. They're stepping closer and closer to her. Oliver brushes her hair with his hand and both Marie and Anna shake her. She won't look at them. Lyle cowers on the swing, rocking back and forth, back, and forth. He's too afraid to talk to her. Only Matthew lingers behind me, watching the scene unfold.

Matthew puts his hand on my shoulder. "It's time, Cara. I need to speak to her." He doesn't look so scary anymore to me, just an old man in a lot of pain and in need of some relief too. "Thank you," he says.

"What will you do?"

"Oh, Cara, don't spoil my fun," he says and winks at me.

"Wait, what does that?"

"Uh, uh, uh, end of the line for you," he says.

He claps his hands twice and I disappear.

When I open my eyes, I'm back in my mother's living room. The bed is still there. Daylight streams through the window, filling it with golden light. I run to the front door and see if Beth's car is still there. It isn't. I pick up my phone and call her, but she won't answer. In seconds, I receive a text that tells me all I need to know, *Cara, just don't. OK?* I think of all the things I could tell her but none of it will change the fact that I can't undo what I've done. I can't force her hand into doing what I want anymore. I settle on texting back: Ok. There are worse things than being ok. I can live with ok. Maybe work my way up to good, eventually, if I'm patient.

I open the sliding glass door to the backyard and walk to the oak tree. My initials are still there, and I finger the curve of the letters. My hand presses into the wood and it's good to feel something so solid, so real. Most of her plants are dead with exception of the mums. Unlike her, I have a black thumb and can't keep any plant alive for more than a week. But the mums? I watered them when I visited her, and they stayed in bloom. Strange, though, as there's already been a frost, but their petals haven't fallen yet. I brush my hands against their soft bloom. Then, a thought. I grab her shovel out of the shed and start to dig and dig and dig. There's an itching feeling I have that I can't shake. I pushed the thought away before, but it hits me stronger now.

What if that whack wasn't a rock at all?

What if, however small, some part of her wanted to tell me this? To face what she did?

Dirt piles up around me. I fling her mums to the left and right and out of my way. I dig and dig and then I hit it, something solid, something round. I shove my hands into the dirt, and I pull it up with all my might. There in my hands is Lyle's little head. Beneath that, a pile of bones. The flesh is long gone. Still, I see a curve of his spine, as if he died holding his head in his knees—crying himself to sleep about Matthew.

Maybe he did.

I gather his bones and zip them into the hospice bed's covering. I'm not quite sure why but it felt like the perfect place to put him, in bed—a place of rest. No more nightmares. No more worries. No more fears of her too. It's ok. It's ok. It's ok. The want of that, the want of his freedom, mine, gave me enough adrenaline to help me drag the bed into the back of Dylan's trunk. My body will curse me tomorrow but for now, I'm ok. I've lifted heavier patients. This will be my final one. The one that releases me from taking care of others for good.

As soon as I get on the road, I call Dylan on speakerphone. When he picks up, I ask, "Where's the best place to buy some kerosene?" He replies, "Oh, hell yeah. But you better be taking me with you."

"I got a story for you this time," I say. "But you're not gonna believe it."

"Ha! Try me. Hey, can you have beers with painkillers? Can we pick some up?"

"Absolutely not."

"What? It'll help the fire, I think."

"I'm hanging up now," I say.

"Ok, ok, ok, but Cara? Is everything... Ok? I know I hit my head hard, but it wasn't that hard right? Like what happened at the house... What did happen at the house? Is Beth ok? Don't tell her I asked about her or it'll get to her head, and I don't need Gumby on speed-dial. Once every full moon is enough for this guy. Trust me."

I can hear the fear in his voice. I was wondering when his jokes would fade away and he'd admit he was worried about me. How lucky I am to have someone who worries about me. Some never live to see that.

"Yes, yes, we're... um, I, she's? Ok."

"You two couldn't even make it a week this time? That's a new record."

I turn into the hospital parking lot and park. "Ok, ok, watch it, buddy. I'll be in soon. Sit tight.

EPILOGUE: HOW WE CARRY ON

Cara

"Oh, not again... Cara, get the thing!" Dylan shouts over the buzz of a hedge trimmer. The sun burns the back of my neck. I wipe sweat out of my eyes and jump out of the back of Dylan's truck with his saw. He mumbles a thank you and curses a rose bush to hell. Most times, Dylan doesn't check out how thick the brush is and jams the trimmer with a branch too thick for the blade to cut. It's been six months of us working side by side and he *still* makes the same mistake every time. But I don't really mind. I like that I know this, that I can anticipate what he will or won't need. At the end of the day, we save fences from being knocked over by trees. We make bushes into animal shapes and round bulbs so that someone can throw a party and say, "How nice."

Of all the jobs in the world, this is one I don't need to take home with me. Sure, Mrs. Harrigan will still leave me a voicemail about how many inches her grass *should* be cut but I don't lose sleep over those details. It's not like it was, not like I was. After we burned the bed in the junkyard, I crushed my work beeper with a hammer. Didn't even give notice. Just one day, I didn't show. I didn't say why or answer any of their calls. I had already answered so many calls for so much of the time. Though I did listen to Susan's voicemail. She thanked me. Was probably a bit concerned that I lit a bed on fire, but seemed to think it was an accident. *Must have been too embarrassed to tell me, huh? Well don't worry hun, you did me a favor, actually.* Turns out, the state wouldn't give her money to replace the hospice bed. But a house fire? Insurance ate that claim up and gave her a brand-new shiny model, one without history or body prints or the bones of a dead boy buried in its seams.

The bones? Dylan scattered them somewhere, mumbling something about some favor and that I couldn't ask more. For once, I didn't. Besides, I don't think Matthew would want the last memory of his son to be of his murder. Who wants that? There'd be no peace from it, just a crappy Netflix docu-series about him.

"Dylan don't forget to clean the teeth," I shout back.
"What?"
I sigh. "Never mind."
"Ok," he bellows. "Almost done. Give me five and time to clean the teeth then we good."

I shake my head and laugh. Most days are like this; incidental. It's better this way. I think I've had enough revelations to last a lifetime. Sometimes I wish Beth could see me like this, brushing things off, letting things go, and carrying on as I can. But I know it's for the best that she doesn't. There are some people that walk into your life and have this way about them. Like they can snap their fingers and revert you to a lesser form, not on purpose, just on muscle memory and nerves. She's like that for me, and that version of Cara, I don't want.

Dylan shuts the hedge trimmers off, and I grab a rake to help him gather the leaves and twigs into a bag. We rake until dusk starts to tumble across the sky. As I toss a handful of leaves into the bag, I relish how tired I am. I'll sleep through the night like a baby—worn, readied to retreat into plush pillows and a down comforter.

The only times I think about her is when I dream.
Not every dream, and not every time.
But sometimes, I see her. When I do, I see the back

of her head. She's walking away from me, and I try to run to catch up. But it won't work. It never works. We're on different tracks and at different speeds, so I can see of her is her leaving. Sometimes, in rare cases, she'll at least turn around to see me as she drifts further. She'll have a look on her face that's halfway between an apology and disappointment. I don't know who let the other down, but I know that that face means it won't change the fact that it's done, and it is what it is. We are what we are. When I wake up, I do my best to cling to that thought. There's no use in wishing for an impossible future. Doesn't mean the wishing doesn't happen. Or that I don't get struck down sometimes with a random thought. That does still happen. But the rawness of it, it's lessened. Before, it the hurt was all I could feel. I truly thought that it'd never end. I wanted to scream—let the world know how I'd never feel whole enough.

But now?

I can go a whole day without thinking of her once. Sometimes, I can go days. I count those as tiny blessings, reminders that I am still here and I'm living for each moment I have. That's all I can do; all anyone can do when faced with a loss. I used to hate when people said trite things like "one day at a time," but in the end, that's all there is, really. A day. Some days. Time. Whatever is of that is mine to use however I see fit. But I'd rather spend my time living for what I have as opposed to living for all I don't. I'm done drinking poison.

"*PJ's?*" I ask Dylan.

"You know it," he says.

Well, not beer. For the love of god, let me at least have beer.

After we finish cleaning up, we hop into the truck and steer onto I-95. I fiddle with Dylan's tapes and put one into the player. *We've only just begun...*starts to play. Dylan jumps up so fast that he hits his head on the roof of the car. "That's a nope," he says, then takes the tape out of the deck and throws it out the window.

"What the?... Dylan didn't your mom give you that?"

He shakes his head. "Fine, I got others she gave me."

"Weirdo," I say, and settle my head against the cool glass of the passenger side window. As we drive, I let my mind drift. My mom loved to garden so the irony of this being my job isn't lost on me. That place that I saw her in, whatever it was, is the last memory I have of her, so I'm sure there's something to that. A therapist would probably say I'm hanging onto her through this and maybe that's partially true. But is that really so bad?

There, it felt like a world between worlds. A place of being and not being at the same time. I don't know if she even remembers speaking to me or really heard me. But I like to think she did. I like to think that she turned away from taking care of all the budding life forms and stopped, just stopped for a moment. Maybe she did stop. Maybe she turned around and faced Matthew. If she tried hard enough, maybe even Lyle would understand her mistake and forgive her. All I know is that given the choice to try and not in this life, she opted out. So, sure, maybe I daydream sometime of her there. When I do, I imagine she faces it all. But I don't imagine that she'll apologize to me anymore. No matter how many times she could have said it then, I know it would never be enough, never feel enough. Deep down, that's not what I wanted either. I wanted what she already told me in that garden, a version of her she'd never be. I'd never get that, nor will I feel what it feels like to have lived a life with that kind of Laurie. I can see now that I wasn't just mourning her, missing her, despite the flaws—I was grieving for the self of me that never had a chance to be. Now and again, I still do mourn that Cara. How can I not? But on days when I'm feeling better, I get to sit in some sunshine, work with my best friend, and crack open a fizzy beer. Some people will never have that, so I try to remember to celebrate the Cara that I've become.

"What are you thinking about? Been real quiet," Dylan says.

"Don't worry about it."

"Uh-huh."

I haven't yet told Dylan about the ghosts; the memory walking, the torture, the garden—mostly it's because whenever I mention it, he puts a hand on my mouth. I think he's afraid that if I talk about it, I'll somehow resurrect them. But they're not coming back. They got what they wanted and one day, when Dylan is way less jumpy, I'll tell him about it. For now, it's my secret to keep.

Isn't that what grief is? Something never known or seen by anyone but you? Even if I try to explain the weight of it all, I can't. As time passes, the loss carries loss. Memories disintegrate. There is just too much of too much. Cracks emerge. I can't control what slips through and what remains. At least, I have this story. I swear, I'll never forget it. The one-time mother became another word for salvation.

CASS CLARKE

Cass Clarke was born in Rhode Island, and, like the smallest state in the U.S., they're made from pint-sized chaos, circuitous directions, and party pizza. They have an MFA from Emerson College in Writing, Literature, and Publishing and fell in love with stories when their dad taught them how to record VHS tapes and use his typewriter. A lifelong horror fan and GALECA critic, their coverage of the genre has been published at Fangoria, Rue Morgue, Dread Central, /Film, Den of Geek, and more. Monthly, they co-host a podcast called Horror Hangover— conducting reviews, interviews, and film analysis. Cass has been a martial artist for over two decades and spends their free time helping children learn the art of Taekwondo. They currently reside with their lil' black dog and spouse in Boston, MA, where they've once again enthusiastically cooked too much food.

ACKNOWLEDGEMENTS

Thanks to the following:

Cat Benstead, Marina Garrido, and the entire Hear Us Scream collective crew for giving me a chance when I'd just about given up telling stories. What a delight they all are and what an honor to join the team!

Ryan, who read every doubt, rant, and email on top of each draft of this story with care and patience, all while being a brand-new parent. Of course, this would be impossible without Betsy—the sweetest there is.

Matt, my cousin, who showed up at the hardest juncture of my life and inspired me to champion empathetic cousins in my story as being the very best sidekicks to get you through the darkest of nights.

Katie, the artist who bound my first finished (but never published) novel, so I could never say I didn't have a book of mine on the shelf and looked at it often to gather the courage to make one to fit alongside it.

Linny, for our truest and lifelong friendship. As I've said before, "Fuck off, you're delightful." Ian is so incredibly lucky to have you as his guiding force and I can't wait to tell him the best ghost stories in the future.

Sarah, my therapist, who could have convinced me that writing a novella instead of taking time off to grieve is a bad idea—but trusted me to work through and with my demons to find my version of peace.

Felice for an incredible book cover that's only rivaled by their committed friendship.

My dojang community for keeping me sane and my roundhouse kicks high.

Tina, Mike, Bonnie, and Ryan for being the best home away from home.

Last on this list but first in my heart, Chris, who makes every day feel possible and loving – even when I want to hide in a blanket fort. You're the best spouse and I couldn't imagine a more fitting partner in my life. Also, haha! I got my haunted house story out before yours! (See, now people will also read yours, too. Smile!)

Printed in the USA
CPSIA information can be obtained
at www.ICGtesting.com
JSHW052105270923
49130JS00024B/270